CW00555959

ROBERT NEEDHAM

This is Where You Fold

The Steve Ash Trilogy: Book 1

First published by Gutshot Publishing 2020

Copyright © 2020 by Robert Needham

All rights reserved. No part of this publication may be reproduced, stored or transmitted in any form or by any means, electronic, mechanical, photocopying, recording, scanning, or otherwise without written permission from the publisher. It is illegal to copy this book, post it to a website, or distribute it by any other means without permission.

This novel is entirely a work of fiction. The names, characters and incidents portrayed in it are the work of the author's imagination. Any resemblance to actual persons, living or dead, events or localities is entirely coincidental.

Robert Needham asserts the moral right to be identified as the author of this work.

Robert Needham has no responsibility for the persistence or accuracy of URLs for external or third-party Internet Websites referred to in this publication and does not guarantee that any content on such Websites is, or will remain, accurate or appropriate.

Designations used by companies to distinguish their products are often claimed as trademarks. All brand names and product names used in this book and on its cover are trade names, service marks, trademarks and registered trademarks of their respective owners. The publishers and the book are not associated with any product or vendor mentioned in this book. None of the companies referenced within the book have endorsed the book.

First edition

This book was professionally typeset on Reedsy.
Find out more at reedsy.com

Contents

Prologue

The Russian parked up in his black SUV, inconspicuously near the target's house. He'd been here a few times before with work, but this was the riskiest job he'd been asked to do so far. He watched the house through the tinted windows of his car, settling in for a long night. He looked over at the passenger seat and double-checked his gun was loaded and ready to go, before screwing a silencer to the front. Although he was playing the part of a hitman, this particular gun was loaded with tranquilliser darts. His objective was to kidnap, rather than kill. His employer had been very clear on that. 'Get the man, get the glasses if you can.' The house was large, the type he'd dreamt about when he'd been younger. It was possibly a four-bed; it was hard to tell from the front. The rain started to fall lightly, and he plugged his earphones into his phone, playing classical music through them to keep his mind sharp.

Around half an hour after he'd arrived, the front door opened and a man in a black raincoat stepped out. His target closed the door quickly and set off, heading down a nearby alleyway. He waited until the target had disappeared from view before slipping out of the SUV, gun in hand, in pursuit. The target was walking at pace, which made it easier to follow him; he was so focused on where he was going that he wasn't thinking about his surroundings. The streets were quiet, so he could take some risky shots if needed.

The Russian increased his pace to get within range. He had to be closer than usual; the tranquilliser dart was less aerodynamic than a bullet, and the silencer was likely to take some of the range off too. As he closed the distance, the Russian lifted his arm, looked down the sights, and aimed. Just as he was about to squeeze the trigger the target turned a corner and disappeared. The Russian ran to the corner, hiding his gun in his trench coat. He was frustrated to see the target was now walking down a residential street, lined with blocks of flats.

He let the distance between himself and the target grow again. This was going to complicate matters. He turned the corner, the gun clamped in his armpit, under his coat. The road ahead curved around one of the blocks of flats. As the target fell out of sight the Russian ran to close the distance again. As he came to the corner he stopped and peered. The target was standing on a bridge over a canal, staring intently at the glasses in his hand. The Russian checked the location on his phone. The towpath ran adjacent to a field. A plan formed in his mind. Shoot the man, hide his body, get the SUV, and get out of there. Nobody was around to see now. He lifted the gun, and pulled the trigger.

A few months earlier…

A Few Months Earlier...

Chapter 1

Steve Ash switched the light on in his garage. It was as unkempt as Steve's hair, with a workbench covered in bits of wire and randomly strewn tools. Several mugs of half-drunk coffee littered the room. His blue Vauxhall Astra was parked outside, and a deconstructed poker table was waiting by the garage door, ready to be loaded into the boot.

Steve pushed the button to open the garage door. There was a soft metallic rattle before the motors groaned into life and the cold morning air broke through the gap. As the door lifted Steve admired the photo of his wife and daughters pinned to the wall. They had been at Forty Hall, a manor house in Enfield. It had felt like years since that photo was taken; the grass was green; the sky was blue, and they all had ice cream that had quickly begun to melt in the heat. His daughters, Ellie, and Fiona were his motivation for life. He couldn't believe that they had already reached eight and six years old. Before they had come along, he had never really tried to do anything out of the ordinary. He'd got a degree, married Tanya, and got a mortgage so expensive that every month, after payday, he was shocked to see most of it immediately go back to the bank.

Shortly after the first few payments, Steve realised he needed to think about generating a second income. Data analysis was steady but unfulfilling, and he'd heard all the horror stories of people made redundant and unemployable at a stroke, after working for the same company for years.

One night, Steve had been at the pub with James, complaining about how bored he was at work. "Well do something different then, mate! We always talked about setting up a business, why don't we do that?" James had replied.

"Yeah but... I dunno, what would we do?" Steve took a swig from his pint glass, the foam starting to dry around the top. He noticed some white spots around the top of his glass where the pub had had the dishwasher on too hot. The pub was nice and modern, with a welcoming atmosphere. There were big wooden tables that encouraged people to share, and after a beer or two inevitably led to people striking up new friendships. In fact, that had been how James and Steve had met. Steve was mightily relieved he'd been able to make friends so quickly after they had moved from London to Hertford. His friends in London, had moved one by one, out of the capital city, the cost of living too much to bear with a growing family. Steve and Tanya had found themselves isolated and leading an expensive lifestyle and moved to get a fresh start.

Steve didn't class himself as an extrovert, particularly, but he'd made an effort to go out and try and make friends and it had paid off. They both knew all the bar staff and had been invited to lock-ins on a regular basis. One of Steve's favourite features of the pub was that it was four minutes from his house, or fifteen minutes if he'd drunk more than his fair share.

"Maybe we could sell birthday cards. I'm fed up of paying a fortune for them, and they can't be that expensive to make."

Steve sighed. "Yeah, but it's not something I'll be able to get passionate about. I barely remember when Tanya's birthday is."

"Well, what are you passionate about?"

"Beer!"

"I know that!" They both took a large gulp of beer as if to prove the point. James finished the half pint of beer he had left in one go and looked at Steve expectantly.

"Come on, get it down you! You've got until I get back with your next pint!" Steve looked reluctantly at the beer in his glass. They'd already had four pints before this one and he was starting to feel a bit queasy. Come on Steve, man up. He let the liquid slide down his throat, shuddering as the contents of the glass emptied into his stomach. James sat back down at the table with two new pints of beer.

"You know what, I really like poker." Steve said, almost as if he was admitting something embarrassing.

"Ha, me too! Why don't we get into the poker business? Actually, Sebastian at work knows a guy that owns a casino. Some guy who throws ridiculous parties in the Bahamas. Alastair... No!" James clicked his fingers, trying to remember the name. "Alexander Jacques. Does his name ring any bells?"

"You know Alexander Jacques?" Steve said, eyes wide. "You're joking! He owns a massive chain of casinos, and I follow him on Twitter. Your friend's right, he does throw ridiculous parties."

"Maybe Sebastian could introduce us."

"OK, so how do we appeal to casinos with this mysterious new poker product?"

"Casinos want people's money, right? So, we need to offer something that helps them make more money."

"Oh my God, I've got it!" Steve shouted, oblivious to the

other customers' stares. He ran to the bar and grabbed some napkins, then drew some shapes; a cylinder, a dotted line and something that looked like a telescope. "We use infrared to see what cards the players have!" Steve looked at James, waiting for the lightbulb to go on in his head.

"OK… and what?"

"We can see what cards the players are playing, so we know which ones are here to gamble and which ones are really conservative. We put the players who are conservative on the same table, and the ones who are loosey-goosey on the other. The casino charges the players a percentage rake on the total pot, so when they build up the player profiles, they can place the gamblers together and keep the conservative players together. That way, they can make more rake from the gamblers."

James raised one eyebrow. "That actually makes sense… Does anyone do that at the moment?"

"I have no idea, although I'm guessing if they did, they'd keep it quiet. It's not the sort of thing you'd want the players to know about."

"All right, I'll text Sebastian now." James sent the text and five minutes later, his phone chimed like a doorbell. "It says, 'I'm meeting up with him in London next Wednesday for a few pints. You're more than welcome to join.'" James beamed at Steve. "We should go!"

Steve looked a bit disappointed. "I can't go, it's parents' evening."

"Can't Tanya go on her own?"

"No mate, she'll kill me if I don't come." Besides, I want to go!

"Guess I'll have to do it on my own, then!"

The drinks with Alexander had gone well, and he'd invited them up to the main casino in Nottingham to demonstrate their idea. Steve had worked his arse off after his day job to build the table and design the software to go with it, and whilst it was all a bit clunky, it worked… just about. Today was the big day. Steve had been up most of the night testing the software. He had managed to steal a few hours' sleep, and it briefly crossed his mind to glug some of the stale coffee to try and wake himself up a bit when the door behind him opened.

Tanya tiptoed barefoot across the concrete garage floor, her pyjamas gently rustling as she went. Her brown hair just touched her shoulders, and she was the same height as Steve, five foot seven. She embraced Steve tightly. "Good luck, baby, I know you can do it."

He squeezed her closer before letting go. "Thank you babe, I feel like I'm running on adrenaline at the moment."

"Just don't let that slimeball run the show. Remember, you made the product he's pitching. You're the brains behind the whole operation. He's just the frontman. You know I don't like him; he thinks he's better than everyone else and he doesn't care about other people's feelings."

"I won't, babe. James is just … over-confident."

"That's one way of describing him." she said, her nose wrinkling. "Have you got everything you need?"

"Yes, just got to load it into the car."

"OK, I'll put the kettle on while you're loading it up." Tanya walked briskly to the door as Steve began putting the boxes in the car. The sun had just broken over the top of the roof of the house on the opposite side of the street when Steve noticed a tall man approaching the house. Even in this light James Baldwin was unmistakable. He walked with the swagger of a man who owned the world, his charcoal three-piece suit tailor-made. Steve by comparison wore a suit that he'd bought from the supermarket. It was a little old, and the fabric near his armpits was starting to wear thin.

"Stevey-boy!" James yelled, at a volume loud enough to wake the entire street. "Are you ready to go and break the bank at Jacques?"

"All right mate, how's it going?" Steve said, blinking.

"You sound like a bag of shit!" James grinned. "Did Tanya have you up all night or something?"

"No mate, I was testing the equipment. I think it's all fine."

"Well, it better be. I've only got one shot at selling to this guy!"

Tanya poked her head around the door "Your coffee's on the side, love!"

"Aw thanks Tanya," James bellowed. "I could murder a brew, but Steve and I had best be off. Don't want to get stuck in traffic on the way!"

A brief look of irritation crossed Tanya's face. "Good luck love, let me know how it goes. I love you."

"I love you too. Call you later." Steve replied. James and Steve got into the blue car, Steve suddenly feeling self-conscious that he hadn't washed it since he'd bought it, before they gently pulled away from the house.

* * *

Rock music started playing, the Bluetooth stereo picking up the last playlist Steve had listened to. "Oh mate, that's going off right away," said James, punching the off button. "I don't know how you can listen to that stuff."

9

"It's better than that autotuned rubbish you like," Steve replied, a broad grin on his face. "They need a computer to do their singing for them!"

"You're sure you've got everything, right?" James asked, suddenly serious.

"Yes mate, I've been up all night doing it. I checked everything several times over." Steve replied, trying his best to look dependable.

"You've definitely remembered the table?"

Steve looked in his rear-view mirror at the enormous felt tabletop he had just about managed to squeeze into the back. "Yeah. I remembered the table." Steve said, with a grin.

"Good. I don't want you messing any of this up. Probably best leave me to do the talking when we get there." James said, looking out of the window. Steve glanced at him. Fat chance of that happening, you don't know how any of it works!

* * *

Three hours later they arrived at the Jacques Casino in Nottingham. Jacques casinos were as luxurious as the casinos in Vegas, with marble walls and floors; and statues built into alcoves in the walls. There was a water fountain at the front of the casino that looked like a large pile of chips, water shooting out of the tallest stacks, and large glass chandeliers hung from the ceiling. This casino also happened to have one of the largest card rooms in the country and had the benefit of being in the middle of the city centre. Steve had played here a few times in tournaments but had only made prize money once, squeaking into the lowest prizes before being knocked out. He hoped today his luck would change.

The meeting was due to take place at 10 am but Steve and James had arrived at 9:30 and were now sitting by the Guest Services desk. A pleasant fragrance filled the air; a mixture of peppermint and cedarwood that helped Steve feel relaxed and invigorated. The adrenaline coursing through his veins was making up for his lack of sleep and he couldn't help but jiggle his leg as they sat in their seats.

"Will you keep still?" James snapped at Steve.

"Sorry mate, I hadn't realised my leg was going. Are you ready?"

"Of course I am. I've just been going through the figures in my head. Are you sure the rakes will go up thirty-five per cent? it still seems like a lot to me."

"I think they'll go up more than thirty-five per cent, but I don't want to overcommit us." Steve looked down at his watch. "It's five to ten, are there any other questions you want to ask me?"

"No, I'm fine thanks." They sat in their seats in silence, and Steve kept looking at his watch. The minute hand hit the one on his watch, and then the two. There was no sign of Alexander, though. I hope we haven't travelled all this way for nothing.

"So, fucking rude, where is he?" Steve heard James mutter under his breath.

At twenty past ten a man in his mid-fifties waddled towards them, his gut so big that he was visibly sweating. He was wearing a black cowboy hat which would have been the right size for most people, but fitted so tightly around the man's skull that it pushed folds of skin down the front of his forehead, making him look like he was frowning. Alexander Jacques, the owner of Jacques Casinos greeted them. It's weird seeing this guy in real life rather than through social media. Don't get starstruck now, Steve!

"Good morning gentlemen, shall we go to my office?" Alexander motioned at a door near the Guest Services desk.

"About time, you fat fuck." James muttered under his breath. Steve jumped out of his seat, but James deliberately took his time, emphasising each movement. They entered a large room that was mostly mahogany, with a desk at one end and a large brown leather sofa facing a wall of TVs, showing CCTV images from around the casino. Alexander sat down and instantly reclined in his leather executive La-Z-Boy chair, which groaned loudly under the strain. Steve and James sat down on the opposite side of the desk.

"So, gents," said Alexander from his reclined position, "you've designed a poker table that you say will help me to make more money in my casinos. How will it do that?"

Steve began to talk before James spoke over him. "It runs on infrared technology. The cards and chips have tiny patterns on the back. They're invisible to the naked eye, but allow you to see the two hole cards each player is dealt from a centralised location."

Alexander leaned forward with an effort and clasped his hands together across the desk, transferring his weight from the chair, and looking bemused. "Infrared is heat-based, isn't it? How do you get the cards to emit heat?"

James leaned forwards in his chair, mirroring Alexander's pose before cutting Steve off from talking again. "It's more of a happy coincidence that heat emits Infrared waves. The table is heated; it's barely noticeable to the players, but it gives off enough energy to warm up the cards and chips, which are designed to concentrate the warmth in the patterned parts. I don't think I've missed anything, have I, Steve?"

"No," said Steve, sulkily. James grinned and sat back in his chair.

Alexander still frowned. "OK, great, so I can read all of the players' cards. Firstly, why do I want to, and secondly, what advantage does this have over the RFID microchips we already have on the tables?"

"Two good questions, both of which I can answer." James replied confidently. "We have designed some software that tracks the hands people have played and shows how conservative they are, or how much they like to gamble. Over time you can build up a profile of each player. When these players come back to the casino, you can group all the gamblers together and keep all the conservative players on one table. Without risk-averse people to keep the pot down, the average pot size will rise much higher on the gamblers' tables. We estimate that the rake from cash tables should go up by thirty-five per cent."

"It's also useful for tournaments," Steve put in, "because if you put the loose players on one table they'll go out faster. Then you can get more re-entries from those players." Steve sat back, pleased to have got a word in.

James shot him a dirty look. "RFID tables aren't reliable; people have worked out how to break their encryption systems, so they can cheat. Even if someone worked out our system it would be nearly impossible to crack, as the IP address transmitting the card information changes every two minutes. We propose telling players that our table can track the colour and the weight of the cards. If people are looking to cheat, then they'll be spending their time trying to break the wrong thing."

Alexander leaned back in his chair and closed his eyes, deep in thought. There was silence in the room, except for the rasp of Alexander's huge chest rising and falling. He opened his eyes. "How much do they cost, then?"

James spoke calmly and clearly, though Steve could see what an effort he was making to control his excitement. "The tables are two thousand pounds each, the software package is a hundred per table per month, including maintenance and software upgrades. The cards are twenty-five pounds per pack, and the chips a hundred per case."

Alexander sighed out one more deep breath, then sat up and stared into James' eyes as if he were trying to see into his soul. He pointed at James, a bead of sweat rolling down his forehead. "I want to see one of these tables in action. If they function well enough, we will trial ten of them in our casino here. If we see an increase in rake to the level you've stated, we will replace the tables across our entire portfolio of casinos." He let those words hang in the air for a moment. "You will receive payment for the tables after the first month, if they are satisfactory."

Steve felt like taking all his clothes off and dancing on top of Alexander's desk. Instead he said, "Perfect, I'll go and get the table."

* * *

Tanya was on her way to Beaumont Lodge, the care home where her dad lived. George was an avid reader of historical fiction and spent most of his time reading and then telling Tanya and Steve all about the backstabbing, scheming, and deception in his latest story. Tanya's mum Josie had died a few years before, having suffered with dementia in her final years. They all missed her; but George had kept his head in his books, and as long as he got to watch the football on a

Saturday afternoon, he seemed content. He had a habit of repeating stories from his younger days many times over, but Tanya didn't mind. He told them with such enthusiasm that she pretended it was the first time she'd heard them.

Tanya was admiring the precision of her parallel parking when her mobile rang. On the screen flashed the word Steve followed by a red heart emoticon.

"Hi baby, how did it go?" she asked, bracing herself for the worst while hoping for the best.

She could hear Steve's excitement in the way he almost fell over his words. "They're buying ten! They're going to put them in all the casinos, and we're going to make a fortune! I love you so much, babe, I can't believe this is happening!"

"Woohoo!" cried Tanya. "That's amazing, I'm so, so proud of you! Well done, baby!" She beamed, though no-one was there to see. "What's the plan now?"

"James and I are just packing the car; we'll head back, then go for a few pints to celebrate." Tanya rolled her eyes. Steve was usually sensible when he went out for drinks, but James had a way of leading him astray, and the last few times they had been out together Steve had come back barely able to walk.

"Well, you deserve it. Keep me updated and enjoy the beers. I'll see you when you get back." she replied, trying not to sound disapproving. Then another thought occurred to her. "I'll get me and the girls a Chinese takeaway to celebrate!" Now *that* was an idea.

* * *

Tanya jumped out of the car and rang the bell at the reception before being buzzed through. Beaumont Lodge was in dire need of some maintenance; the paint was peeling and the floor scuffed. There was a lingering smell of roast meat that reminded Tanya of school dinners. But it was the best they could afford, and the staff had always treated Dad well. She knocked on his door and heard a faint 'Just a minute'. Then the door opened. There stood Dad, green jumper neat and yellow tie precisely knotted, as smart as ever. He seemed to have shrunk again.

"Hello, love," he said, "I wasn't expecting to see you today."

Tanya gave him a big squeeze. "Are you eating your dinners, Dad?"

"Ah well, you know, I'm never that hungry these days. What have you got there, love?" George asked, reaching out for the book in her hand. Tanya smiled as her dad's face lit up at the cover.

"Conn Iggulden? I didn't know this had come out! Thank you very much!" Then he paused. "Err, it is for me, isn't it?"

"Of course it is, you silly bugger!" Tanya said, laughing. They sat down in a pair of old armchairs; the leather cracked from years of use. "So, what's new, Dad?"

"Not much. Enid died a few days ago. How about you, love? How are the kids? Is Steve all right?" He shifted in his chair.

"Ellie and Fiona are fine, but the big news is with Steve." Tanya grinned. "His big meeting in Nottingham went well, and they're buying ten of his new tables."

"Oh, that's fantastic, I bet he's well chuffed."

"Yeah, he is." Then Tanya frowned. "But I'm worried, the guy he's gone into business with is a bit of an arsehole. He thinks he's better than everyone and if I'm honest, I think he bullies Steve. It's great that he's had success and I want to... No, I *will* support him. I just wish he'd been able to do this with someone

16

else. I don't know why, but I think he's going to end up with a raw deal. I can feel it in my waters." Tanya remembered her mum saying that she could feel it in her waters when she was predicting the next couple to leave *Strictly Come Dancing*.

Dad smiled. "Well, I won't argue with your waters. But don't worry too much, I'm sure it will all be fine. Why don't we go for a walk, to take your mind off it?"

Tanya managed to keep calm through the walk, the school run, and their celebratory takeaway. But once the girls were in bed, she watched the hands of the clock crawl round, and wondered when Steve would make an appearance.

Chapter 2

One month had passed. Steve was sleep-deprived and exhausted, but it had been worth it. He had quit his job, and rather than go out in a blaze of glory, as he had pictured himself doing, he agreed to work his two weeks' notice. He spent the following three weeks negotiating a deal and project-managing the building and shipping of tables to Jacques Casino with the company who had built their prototype.

He had agreed with James that they would each invest £65,000 into the business – which was twenty thousand more than Steve and Tanya had in savings. Steve had decided that it would be best not to tell Tanya about the extra £20K, and had instead borrowed the money from a loan website called Dosh.com, who charged an exorbitant interest rate but had an easy form to fill out. Steve hated forms. Besides, he was confident that he could pay it back before anyone needed to find out.

James had been busy, too. He had made patent applications for the tables and the software and set up the business with Companies House. In fact, one of the first things James had done was make himself CEO of Baldwin and Ash Gaming Tables Ltd, appointing Steve, much to his own amusement, as company secretary. He wondered whether Steve would ever bother to check the documents and decided to keep his joke to himself for the time being. The software that Steve had developed to work with the tables was a thing of beauty, and James had to give him credit for linking the two together so seamlessly. He had expected the patents process to be long and drawn out, but "pending" status had been granted surprisingly quickly. Somehow James had missed Steve's name off the application, since it hadn't been obvious that you could put two names in the applicant section. Of course, he *would* get around to amending the application – but then again, Steve wasn't going to check.

Alexander Jacques had quickly passed the project off to some guy called Eddie, who in turn had handed it over to Brian Bellamy, the manager of the Nottingham casino, much to James' irritation. Brian was very keen to show what he could do; his boss Eddie was a hard man to impress at the best of times, and he wanted to prove that he was area manager material. Consequently, he had called James twice a day to check in on progress, and once the tables had arrived, disappeared off the face of the earth.

Despite several attempts to reach Brian, James only managed to get hold of him four weeks after all ten tables had been delivered, by ringing up as Alexander Jacques. He could hear the receptionist on the tannoy: 'Message for Brian, call from Mr Jacques.' James could almost hear Brian's footsteps thudding across the casino before his breathless greeting. "Hi, Alex … how … was the … Bahamas?"

What a brown nose. "Hello Brian, you slippery sod! I've been trying to get in touch with you for ages. It's James from Baldwin and Ash Gaming Tables. How are the tables doing?"

"Oh … hi James." Brian didn't hide his disappointment well. "Yeah, y'know, they've been all right, the felts are nice."

"Never mind the felts, talk to me about the rakes. Have they gone up?"

"Yeah, a bit, but it's hard to say if it's the tables. We've had some big promotions on, loyalty points for re-entries in the tournaments and free soft drinks if you're playing cash, and that's really brought the punters in. I reckon that's what's done it." Brian said confidently.

James wasn't having any of it. "Come on then, Brian, how much have the rakes gone up?" he snapped. "Our contract says that if the rakes go up by twenty per cent, we get tables in across the country. Give me the numbers."

"Um, they've gone up sixty-two per cent," Brian mumbled. "Like I said, though, we've had some great incentives running for the players."

"Sixty-two per cent?" James shouted. "Brian, where have you been with this information? We ought to sue you for keeping that to yourself. I've half a mind to ring Alexander up right now." James didn't have Alexander's personal number, since Sebastian wouldn't share it and for some reason Alexander hadn't given it to him, which James had dismissed as a multimillionaire's eccentricity. Brian, however, wouldn't know that.

"Really?" squeaked Brian. "Oh my God. I'm so sorry. I didn't know… Please don't ring Alex! What do you need? Tell me what you need."

James was glad this conversation was happening on the phone, since he was grinning from ear to ear. "This is what I need, Brian. I need you to get rid of any tables that aren't ours and replace them with ones ordered from me. What's the name of your area manager again?"

"It's Eddie," Brian quavered.

"Great. Once I get off the line, you're going to phone Eddie and tell him how good the tables are, and recommend he gets them in all the other casinos. If I don't have an order in the next week, expect to be hearing from our lawyers." James paused to let his message sink in. "Understood?"

Brian gulped. "Understood. I'll do it."

"Good." James hung up and smiled to himself. What a good day's work. He had managed to sweet-talk the CEO of the biggest casino firm in the country to buy *his* product. Then he'd chased the follow-on sales *and* got them. Sure, Steve had made the tables, but that was really all he'd done. Any manufacturer could do that. Surely that wasn't worth half the profits. *Steve's nice enough, but he's starting to be an embarrassment. Look at how he tried to muscle in on my pitch... And he's such a wimp.* The germ of an idea entered James's head, and he stood up abruptly. *That's worth thinking over at the pub.*

* * *

The following day, Steve called James for an update. He had just paid the first instalment of his loan, which had underlined the reality of his decision.

"Hi mate, have you heard back from the casino yet? It's been four weeks."

"Hi Steve. You've actually timed it well; I've just got off the phone with them." James sighed. "Listen, it's not gone how we'd hoped; I think it's best we meet up and talk face to face. Shall I meet you at the pub around seven?"

"Oh... Yeah OK, I'll meet you there then."

Steve paced, unsettled, and decided to watch some replays of the European Poker Championship on YouTube. The first replay he chose was day three of EPC Prague, and Dylan Broadmoor was playing on the feature table. He was a brash Hawaiian shirt-wearing American, who thought he was God's gift to the world, and was notorious for having a short temper when he lost. He was holding a particularly good hand against a player the commentators had nicknamed 'The Gorilla', presumably because he had a big bushy beard and long hair as opposed to having a fondness for bananas. Dylan had Ks Jh and The Gorilla had 7h 8h.

The flop ran out Jd 4s 4h, giving Dylan two pairs, jacks and fours, and a king kicker. The Gorilla only had a pair of fours but decided to bet. Dylan called.

The turn was the 10h, a good card for The Gorilla as it gave him a gutshot straight draw, as a 9 on the river would give him a straight, and a flush draw, as any heart would give him a flush. He bet again. Dylan frowned. "I don't think you have anything," and called.

The river was the 9d, giving The Gorilla the best hand with a straight of J, 10, 9, 8, 7, versus Dylan's two pairs J, J, 4, 4, K. The flush, which was the most likely hand The Gorilla could have improved too, was missed. Now, The Gorilla bet big.

"Are you trying to blast me off with a missed flush here?" said Dylan, looking ruffled. "I don't think you bet that on the flop. God, I hate poker sometimes. What the hell do you have?" He paused, thinking. "Maybe you have queens, or ace jack. I know that I'm losing but I can't fold. Heck, I call." He nudged the chips over the line of the table.

The Gorilla turned his cards over. Out of the camera line, someone said "Oh My God!"

Dylan jumped out of his chair, red-faced. "This fucking guy comes here and tries to give me all of his chips! I can't believe you were bluffing me all the way and then got there on the river. This is *so* fucking sick." He pointed an accusing finger. "How do you bet on the flop? You are a terrible player. I will play you heads-up any time you like, you moron. Just let me know the time and the place." His voice had risen to a shout. Dylan Broadmoor sat back down in his seat and nonchalantly knocked an apple off a table next to him onto the floor. The rest of the table looked at each other, and began to laugh, first quietly, then out loud.

Steve laughed along with them. *What an idiot!* He watched a few more hours of the footage, and temporarily forgot his worries.

* * *

James arrived at the pub first, feeling nervous for the first time in years. He hesitated. *Should I do this, or should I keep a clear head?* The butterflies in his stomach resurfaced and James ordered two sambucas and two pints of Doom Bar ale, his and Steve's favourite tipple. The pub was quiet; the only other customer was an old man in the corner who seemed a part of the furniture. James slammed both shorts, then took the beers over to a table. He got the contracts out, placed them where Steve would sit, and sighed out a deep breath. He placed his phone on the table and began mindlessly scrolling through Facebook and Twitter, not taking in any of the content. He noticed his armpits were damp and he tried casually to let the air circulate around them, though he knew he must have looked a bit weird holding them at a forty-five-degree angle.

Come on, dry up. The last thing I need to do is sweat buckets.

He had just composed himself when Steve came in. "Hi, mate," James said, in as glum a voice as he could manage, He followed up with a pull at his beer.

"Hi James, what's the news?" Steve said, sitting down at the table. He didn't seem to have registered James's tone.

"Well, Jacques liked the tables, but they've asked to renegotiate the contracts. They did improve their rake, but only by 25% so they've asked us to come down in price. They want us to halve the software fees." He drank again. "That said, they'll order tables for Nottingham, Leicester and Birmingham if we agree. So, I think we should do it." He put his drink down on the table with a clunk.

"Ok, well that doesn't sound so bad." Steve said, with a smile. "I'm happy to go with that too. I assume I just need to sign the contract, and then we're good to go?"

"Yeah," mumbled James, not looking at him. "There's two copies, and you need to sign both."

Steve opened the first contract and wrote his initials at the bottom of the page before quickly turning over and doing the same on the next page. James watched, intent, as Steve initialled all the pages and scribbled his name on the last page. "Now the other one," he said, not taking his eyes off Steve until he signed the second contract.

"Nice one mate," he said. "One copy for me, if you would." He held out a hand, and Steve put a set of papers into it. "I'll be honest with you; I feel like death warmed up. Do you mind if I go home?"

Steve shot him a surprised glance. "Aren't you going to finish your beer?" Then he laughed. "You must be ill."

"No, I really don't feel great," said James and Steve felt bad for joking about it. "I'll head off now."

"You do that," said Steve. "How about we catch up tomorrow, and work out how we go about distributing the tables to the other casinos?"

"Let's do that," James said, getting up with his copy of the contract clutched in his hand. "See you then."

James walked slowly until the pub door had closed behind him. Then he ran to the nearest taxi rank. His new flat was waiting for him, and he had some last-minute packing to do.

Chapter 3

Steve walked home. It was drizzling, and he felt fine rain settling on him without really making him wet. The streetlights illuminated puddles in the pavement, and as he walked, he thought about the evening. James had seemed odd; unusually reserved and quiet. *Has he told me the whole story?* But maybe he really was just ill and not in the mood to celebrate. The news that the casino wanted to take on more tables had felt strangely anti-climactic. *I thought I'd feel like I'd made it, but it was kind of what I expected all along.* Then he smiled and shrugged. *But I'd have been devastated if it had gone the other way.* Steve turned the corner onto his street and saw the lights of his house glowing brightly. *Everyone's home.* He opened the front door and heard quick, light footsteps in the living room.

Tanya appeared a moment later. She was wearing her blue elephant pyjamas, which Steve had bought for her the previous Christmas. Every night, Tanya and the kids had a pyjama party; they got into their pyjamas, put some music on and danced for ten minutes in the living room before the girls sat down with a glass of milk and a cookie before bed. Initially it had started as an incentive to get the kids ready for bed, but it had become an Ash household tradition. Tanya was rosy-cheeked and glowing, but already had a sympathetic look on her face, as if expecting bad news. "So how did it go?"

"Amazing," Steve replied, and was surprised by the flatness of his tone. "They want to fit tables in three more casinos. Nottingham, Leicester and Birmingham."

"That's amazing! I'm so proud of you!" Tanya hurried over and flung her arms round Steve, ignoring his damp clothes. They walked through into the kitchen, their favourite room, and the heart of the home. Tanya was a keen baker and had many happy memories of making cakes with the children. Steve liked the six-ring gas hob, which was built into an island in the middle of the kitchen and accessible from both sides, allowing him to sneak spoonful's from the pan when Tanya's back was turned. The kitchen was Tanya's domain, and a far cry from Steve's messy garage. The long wooden table was clean and tidy. The oven, also in the central island under the hob, was immaculate. Steve threw the contract on the table and sat down, and Tanya made cups of tea. "So, what's this?" she asked, eyeing the paperwork.

"They asked us to come down on some of the costs," said Steve. He sipped his tea, but it didn't quell the faint uneasiness in his stomach. "The revenue from their rakes didn't go up as much as we had told them it would."

"Do you mind if I have a quick look?" Tanya said, and picked up the contract. She leafed through, skimming it. Then she came to a section headed *Structural Changes to Baldwin and Ash Gaming Tables Ltd* and began to read more slowly. Steve watched her read, and her intent expression deepened into a frown. "Have you read this?" she asked, putting the contract down on the table.

Steve swallowed. "Um, kind of."

"Including this?" Tanya stabbed a finger at the middle of a page. "'Steve Ash agrees to release all equity in the business including any funds he has contributed.'?" Her voice shook. "Steve, tell me you didn't agree to this?"

"I know the fees we're charging are lower, but it's still a good deal." Steve said. "Isn't it?"

"But this says you're giving up your entire stake in the company and everything you've put in! All our savings!" Tanya breathed hard. "Is that a good deal?" she shouted.

"Where does it say that?" Steve snatched up the contract and read. There it was, in plain black text." A wave of nausea broke over him. "I'm sure it's just a misunderstanding," he said, and his throat was dry. "James wouldn't do that. I'll ring him. I'm sure he's just messing about." He got out his mobile and rang James's number, pacing while he waited for the call to connect. After two rings, the phone went straight to voicemail, and Steve's heart hit the floor. He turned to Tanya, whose face was flushed with anger.

"You didn't read it, did you?" Her hands were clasped together in a tight fist.

"Of course I did babe." Steve took a step back. "I must have missed that page."

"You liar!" Tanya cried. "Of course you haven't read it! He's made you the company secretary; you're not even a director!" Steve looked down at the floor, and felt tears rolling down his face. He had never experienced a sinking feeling quite like this before.

"If there is anything else you haven't told me, you'd better come clean. Now." Steve felt as if her words were piercing his skull. He tried to look at his wife, but he couldn't meet her eyes.

"I took out a loan," he said, the last word a sob. "To put into the business."

"How much." Tanya's voice showed no emotion.

"Twenty thousand. Well, now it's twenty-two, with interest..." Tanya didn't reply. The moment stretched between them. Finally, Steve steeled himself, and made eye contact. He had never seen Tanya look so angry.

"Get out," she said, very quietly. Steve didn't move; he felt as if he were frozen to the spot. The only thing that could move were the tears coursing down his face. "GET OUT!" Tanya screamed, standing up and flinging an arm at the door. Steve grabbed his keys and bolted. He seized his coat, knocking one of the kids' coats to the floor in the process. He didn't stop to pick it up – he couldn't – and slammed the door in his haste to leave. Steve got into the car and headed straight to James' flat, his usual careful approach to driving gone. His whole body was overcome with rage. As he turned the corner into James's street, he hit a puddle and soaked a pedestrian. The man shook a fist and swore, but Steve didn't stop to apologise.

He reached James' apartment block and pulled up onto the pavement, parking diagonally. He got out, charged at the main door of the block, and leaned on James's buzzer. A dial tone came out of the speaker, like a phone ringing. Steve waited, and the rain began to pick up. The dial tone stopped. No answer. *Fuck this*. Steve tried all the buttons, ignoring any questions, until someone buzzed him in. He ran up the stairs, adrenaline coursing through his veins, till he reached the third floor. *James lives in 36, doesn't he?* He ran, counting *...thirty-four ... thirty-five...* He reached the right door, and lifted his fist to bang on the door –

A sheet of paper was taped to the door. Steve tore it off, and

29

read.

Steve, when you get this note you'll have read the contract. I'm sorry things had to end this way, but you were holding me back, just like Tanya holds you back. No hard feelings, mate.

Steve screwed the note into a ball, and yelled at the top of his voice. He was too furious for words. He dialled James's number again, and it went straight to voicemail. This time he left a message "James, don't do this to me," he gasped. "You're putting me and Tanya in terrible debt and I don't know how I'll pay it off." He tried to choke back his tears. "At least give us our savings back. Call me." He ended the call, and stared at his silent phone.

* * *

Tanya picked up the phone, her whole body trembling, and dialled her dad's number. It rang for a few seconds, then she heard Dad fumbling with the receiver. "Hello?" He sounded surprised.

"I knew it, Dad, I knew something bad would happen. Steve's lost the business." she said, fighting to keep back the tears.

"How on earth did he do that?"

"His *arsehole* of a partner put it in the contract. Steve's left with all of the debt, and none of the business … and he signed it!" she cried, barely able to believe it herself.

"But why would he sign something like that?" said George. "Is he mad?"

"He didn't even read it!"

"Bloody hell, what an idiot," George sighed, "So what are you going to do now, darling?"

"I don't know, Dad. Our savings have gone, and he owes a

lot of money." Tanya sighed. She knew this would be hard for her dad to hear. He'd want to help, but he was using the money from the sale of his house to pay for his care home, and that was depleting quickly... They had sold the house ten years ago, and Tanya didn't know how much of the money was left. She didn't want her dad to move; he had a good group of friends there and she didn't know if he'd be able to start again at the age of 87.

"Listen, you should take some of the money from the house —"

"We can't, Dad. You need that, and we might have to move you if that money runs out." Tanya shook her head. "I just don't know what to do."

* * *

Steve drove up the M1. The rain pounded against the windows, almost the only sound on the quiet road. *How could I have been so naive? And how could James be such a backstabbing shit?* He had no way to get the rage out of his system other than randomly screaming and thumping the steering wheel. *How could James do this to me? We've been friends for ever, and I've always been there for him.*

Steve put his foot down and watched the needle on the speedo glide towards ninety. The Astra groaned, but Steve ignored it, moving into the outside lane. Then a flash as he drove under a road sign. *Fuck*, Steve thought. *Just what I need, my first speeding ticket.* He slowed down, even more annoyed with himself. Another road sign: *Luton 6. Isn't there a Jacques Casino in Luton?* Steve took the next exit.

* * *

Luton is horrible, Steve thought as he drove through the outskirts of the town. He took a left off the main road into a retail park. Brightly coloured neon lights glowed in the night sky, *Carnival Bingo* on the left, *Burger King* on the right, and *Jacques Casino* shone bright red in the middle. Steve parked the car and walked to a cash machine. He checked the balance of his personal account: just over a thousand pounds. *Do you require any other services?* asked the cash machine. *Do I?* thought Steve. He pulled his phone from his pocket and rang Tanya, but she didn't pick up. Steve shrugged, and punched *Yes, Cash without receipt,* and *£200.*

Steve walked into the casino and showed his membership card. He hadn't played poker himself for a while, though he'd lurked, watching players, for research purposes. He thought he had good enough basic knowledge to play successfully in a £1-£2 cash game. He preferred tournaments really, but registration for the evening tournament had already closed. He hoped that maybe he could pick off some of the people who had lost early and were feeling tilted.

In comparison with Nottingham, the Luton Jacques Casino looked tired and run down. Tinny tunes tinkled from the slot machines and Steve spotted two old ladies who had commandeered two machines each, pulling the levers on both like some sort of bizarre cross-trainer. They had *Reserved* signs next to them, ready to stop anyone jumping on their machine when they went for a break.

Steve walked up to the poker desk. "Can I join a one-two game, please?"

"We have a seat on two tables, which would you prefer?"

asked the room manager. Steve checked the two tables. One was heavily dominated by old men who Steve assumed would be cautious spenders, while the other one held a mixture of people, whom Steve assumed had been knocked out of the tournament. He decided to take the seat at that table; if he won big, he could start paying some of his debt off.

"Hi, everyone," Steve said as he sat down. He got a few hellos back, but his table didn't look like it was going to be chatty. That came as a bit of a relief; Steve didn't feel much like talking. He was immediately dealt in, in middle position. Steve looked at his cards, trying not to lift them too far off the felt. It was an easy first decision, as he threw 9s 2h into the muck and looked round for a valet. He needed caffeine. Eventually a valet wandered over to the table and he ordered a coffee. When she returned, he dropped a £1 chip onto the valet's tray in the hope she would turn up little faster next time.

It took a full three orbits before Steve decided to play a hand; the last thing he wanted to do was lose the two hundred pounds in front of him. He looked down at 5s 6s and limped from middle position, calling the £2 big blind. Three people limped behind him, a drunk man with a bald head, ginger beard and a thick Scottish accent, a young guy in a green hoody, and a lady in her seventies who seemed to tremble with the effort of putting her chips in. The action was now on a scruffy man in a suit who decided to raise. "It's too cheap. Let's make it a tenner," he said, throwing in two red chips with £5 written across them in bright gold. The small blind, an Asian man who seemed to be constantly on the phone, and the big blind, a young lady with blonde hair, both folded. *Here we go*, thought Steve, and tossed in two £5 chips. The three limpers behind him also called, making the pot £53 in total.

The flop was dealt. 4s 7s Kh

Holy shit, what a flop! I could make a straight or a flush if I stick around Steve thought as he checked, hoping the scruffy guy in the suit would bet. It checked around the table before he did exactly that, betting £30. Steve called, as did the young man in the green hoodie, and the Turn card was dealt.

As

Bingo! Steve smirked. *Wrong room for that.* He checked and the scruffy man bet £45 into the £143 pot. Steve tried to sound calm as he announced, "All-in" and pushed his chips forward. The young man took a long sad look at his cards before he folded, and the action was with the scruffy man in the suit.

"Fuck's sake!" the man cried, looking at his cards one last time in the hope that they had changed. "Well, that was a shit turn for King Queen." he said, throwing his cards into the muck. Steve scooped the chips in, delighted. He threw a few £1 chips back to the dealer, who picked them up, tapped them twice on the felt to show the cameras above they were a tip, then pushed them through a hole in the table to a safe below. Steve smiled briefly, before remembering what had led him to being in the casino.

* * *

Steve played a few more hands, losing some, winning some. His stack was down to £270 when he looked down at the Ah Ad, the best starting hand in poker. Steve raised to £10 and was immediately called by the drunk Scot to his left. He had been shouting across to one of his friends, who was still in the tournament. He reminded Steve slightly of Dylan Broadmoor.

The action folded round to the scruffy man whom Steve

had played before, who had been complaining about his bad luck. He had made it very clear he was losing, and it sounded as though he had rebought once already after losing all his chips. Steve could not have been happier when he heard him say "Raise". He made it £30 to play and the action folded back around to Steve, who decided to call and see if he could let the guy blast his chips off. The Scot to his left, seemingly only capable of talking at maximum volume, bellowed "Fuck it, in for a penny in for a pound!" threw his chips in, and sunk some lager, spilling some down the corner of his mouth.

The flop came down – Js Qs 9h – and Steve checked. The Scot chucked £30 over the line, grunting as he slopped more beer over himself. The man in the suit called, and it came back around to Steve. *I wish I could see what they've got.* Steve calculated the pot – £153 – and thought about all the turn cards that could make his pair of aces suddenly weak. Any spade could give someone a flush; any king, 10 or 8 could give someone a straight. He wanted to make sure he got as much value as he could, and he didn't want to scare them off. In the end, Steve decided the money in the pot was good enough, and declared himself all in.

The drunk stared at Steve in disbelief. "Have you been hiding a wee monster under the bed?"

The dealer, a small blonde girl, intervened. "Sir, this is a multiway pot. No talking, please."

"Oh aye, sorry love," he said, chuckling to himself. "Go on then, pal, I'll give you a spin." Steve hadn't played a lot of poker recently, but phrases like that filled him with dread. The man in the suit sighed, had another look at his cards and reluctantly made the call as well.

"You're all about to see how unlucky I am," he said, for the fiftieth time that evening. Steve didn't need the loud cheering of the Scotsman, or the fact that he had turned over the 8s 9s before the hand had finished, to know that he had just lost all his money on the 5s turn. The 2h on the river didn't make any difference. Steve threw his cards into the muck before the guy in the suit turned over Ac 9d for third pair. "Look at this rubbish…" Steve heard him say as he got up from the table.

Steve stared at the carpet as he trudged to the exit, the lights of the slot machines seeming much dimmer than on the way in. He felt the judgemental gazes of the two old women as he walked past them, not daring to look up and make eye contact. *Everyone in the casino knows I'm a loser. An embarrassment.* Shame gripped his stomach like a vice. He drove home, only stopping at an off-licence for a bottle of whisky.

Chapter 4

T*ap tap tap...*
Steve's bottle of whisky hit the floor of the car as he awoke sharply. His head was pounding, and he felt as if he was going to throw up. Tanya was peering in at the window.

"I am still very angry, but the kids can't see you sleeping in the car with a half-drunk bottle of whisky." She rolled her eyes. "There's a cup of coffee for you on the kitchen table, I suggest you get inside." Then she marched back into the house.

Steve bent to pick up the bottle slowly glugging its contents onto the floor. Any sleepiness was quickly blasted away as he accidentally pushed the car horn with the top of his head, almost giving himself a heart attack in the process. He looked around to see if anyone had heard, but the street was quiet in the summer sunshine. Feeling sorry for himself, Steve wandered inside, sat down at the kitchen table, and put his head in his hands. Tanya was getting the kids ready for school and he could hear their pattering footsteps. Steve managed a slurp of coffee before Ellie saw him. She ran over and squeezed him as tightly as she could.

"Pooh, Daddy you stink!" she said, pinching her nose and running to grab her school bag. Steve couldn't help but chuckle; *I probably do stink*, he thought. He sighed, and his thoughts drifted back to the last hand he had played the night before, replaying each decision in his mind. *Should I have raised more to start with? Should I have three-bet pre-flop? Or maybe I should have just called on the flop, then reassessed on the turn. It would have been so much easier if I'd known what cards they all had. How on earth am I going to explain this to Tanya?* Steve suddenly felt incredibly hot. *Here come the alcohol sweats,* he thought. The kids put their shoes on quickly; an unusual occurrence, and one which Steve was extremely grateful for.

"Have you got everything?" Tanya shouted down the stairs.

'Yes!' they replied in unison.

"See you later, girls, have a great day," Steve said, walking over to the front door to wave them off. Once they had left, he went back into the living room and fell asleep on the sofa. The next thing he heard was Tanya's key in the door. He rolled himself upright and went to meet her.

"I'm so sorry, baby." Tanya took her flip flops off without answering. Then she walked through into the kitchen and switched the kettle on. Steve followed, not knowing what else to do. Tanya turned to face Steve as the kettle groaned into life.

"Last night I had to make a decision about whether or not I could continue with this marriage. If you lie to me, Steve, how am I supposed to trust you?" Steve had no answer to that. Tanya leaned against the worktop. "I have to think about the children as well as myself, and it would devastate them if we broke up."

"It would devastate me as well, babe." Steve said, his bottom lip trembling.

Tanya sighed. "Have you managed to speak to James?"

"The first thing I did after I left was go over to James' place. He's vanished, but he went to the trouble of leaving a note on the door for me. He's obviously been planning this for some time." Steve threw the crumpled ball of paper over to Tanya, who unfolded it and scanned the contents.

"I don't hold you back! What a bastard!" she yelled. She looked up at Steve, and looked as if she was going to shout at him too, then seemed to calm down. "We need to work out what we're going to do to get out of this hole. I'm not breaking up with you, but you have a *long* way to go before we're back to the way things were."

Steve let out a huge sigh of relief. "I'll do everything that I can. I'll look for a job, I'll see if I can do some contracting, and try to make some money back on the loan. I *will* get us out of this."

"I should think so," said Tanya sternly. "Where did you get the loan from?"

Steve shuffled his feet. "Please don't judge me too harshly… I got it from Dosh.com."

"You idiot," Tanya said, shaking her head. Steve looked at the floor. "Send me the details and I'll see if I can get you onto a plan that charges less interest." She knew Steve had really messed up, but despite it all, she still loved the man sitting at the kitchen table. She walked over to him and placed a hand gently on his arm. "We'll be all right, you know." He looked up at her, the tears welling up in his eyes. "One step at a time, Steve. Go and have a shower, and we can work things out after that." Steve went for a shower and then headed to the office, where he found Tanya smiling at the screen of the family computer.

"Right, I've found a deal that charges two per cent a year

rather than ten per cent a month, and I've borrowed that money under my name as I have a better credit rating. I've also deferred the start of the loan, so we have a few months to get back on our feet. You'll have to pay me back about £300 per month in three months' time. If we start shopping at discount stores, we can squeeze £100 from there. It's still a lot of money... but it's better than £2000 per month."

"Oh babe, thanks for doing that. That's a huge weight of my mind already." *Why didn't I just ask her sooner? I can't let her lose the money, though. This is my fault, and I should be the one paying it off...*

"Right, you need to log into your dosh.com account and I'll pay it back. Then you need to write your CV up and start sending it out to employers." Steve did as he was told, logging into his account on the family computer before fetching his laptop and opening his CV. The last few months were going to be hard to explain... He felt anger rising inside him, consuming him like the flame of a bonfire.

"Fuck!" he yelled at the top of his lungs, and banged the table before composing himself. *No point getting angry; I should have been more careful.* As Steve was composing an entry for April to June, Tanya hurried into the kitchen. "I'm late for work! You know what the nursery is like if you don't get there fifteen minutes early! They'll have me changing nappies all day. If you pick the kids up, I'll see if I can do overtime."

"Sure," said Steve. He swallowed. "I'm so sorry about all this, babe..."

"Look, it is what it is. We'll work things out." Tanya replied, slinging her bag across her shoulder. Steve watched her go. *How did I get so lucky?* He spent the rest of the morning on job applications, then decided to make himself a coffee as a reward. His favourite mug was in the garage. He fetched it and, as he was about to leave, he spotted a deck of cards he had made for the infrared cameras. Steve put the mug down on his workbench and picked the cards up, tracing his finger across the area on the back of the cards where the patterns were hidden.

A thought popped into his head. *I probably could see these cards...*

* * *

Steve tried to focus on completing more job applications, but his mind kept wandering back to the cards. The cameras they had provided with the tables were essentially night-vision goggles. He obviously wouldn't be able to wear those in a casino without rousing suspicion, but maybe... *Maybe I could make a pair that look like normal glasses...* Eventually the thought blocked everything else out, so Steve began to investigate. After typing what felt like hundreds of different phrases into Google, he came across a research article from an Australian university. At the top was a photo of a pair of sunglasses which had a thin layer of nanocrystals. They converted infrared to show warmer colours in red light, and cooler colours in blue. They looked pretty good, too. But they wouldn't be for sale, since they were a prototype; Steve would need to make them himself. The film was made from aluminium gallium arsenide, which was going to be a problem. It had many benefits for what he was trying to do, and was more efficient at picking up the wavelengths, but it was incredibly expensive, and the molecule structure was unstable. *It'll have to be silicon, and I'll just have to hide the circuits within the frames of the glasses.* Steve watched a few videos on YouTube, made himself another coffee, then went into the garage and began to deconstruct an old phone.

* * *

It took a couple of weeks before Steve managed to make a pair of glasses that worked. That was partly due to lack of materials, but mostly because he had done his share of the school runs, and taken a supervisor job at Lyle's Supermarket.

Steve tried the glasses on again and sighed. He'd had to build a miniature computer within the frame, which made the glasses bulky, and heavier than he had expected. He'd wanted them to look like sunglasses, but he looked more like a computer nerd from the eighties. Still, they worked, and didn't look suspicious. Steve picked them up from the workbench, testing them again. As he placed them on his nose, he felt the two buttons on the inside of the frame depress and the word '*Loading*' flashed up on the lenses in big red letters. Eventually the word vanished, and the lenses became clear again. He walked over to the opposite side of the room, where he'd pinned all 52 playing cards to a corkboard in four rows. He looked at the top row and scanned across from left to right. As 2s 3s…

Steve took the glasses off, and grinned. *Time to make some real money*, he thought.

Chapter 5

"Are you sure you'll be all right on your own?" asked Tanya.

"Of course I will," said Steve, laughing. "Hurry up, or you'll never get to Blackpool before their bedtime! You know what Friday traffic's like." He walked to the foot of the stairs. "Come on, kids, time to get in the car."

Tanya's sister's invitation to spend the weekend with her in Blackpool couldn't have come at a better time. Steve couldn't go, because he had a shift on Saturday, but he didn't mind at all. A tournament was taking place at Jacques Casino in Birmingham on Friday evening; £30 to play, and a £4000 guarantee. Steve smiled to himself, thinking back on the first tournament he'd played. *I turned up thinking the guarantee was the amount first place was going to get, not the prize pool split amongst the top 13%. Still, at least the prizes go up in increments; I reckon first will be about £800.* Steve figured he could lose thirty pounds if the glasses didn't work out, and it wouldn't even be noticed.

He kissed Tanya and the girls goodbye, waved them off, and gave them fifteen minutes in case they came back for something. Then he set the sat nav on his phone for Jacques Casino, Birmingham. Just under two hours to get there. The sun was high in the sky; he had plenty of time. Steve got into the car, then jumped back out and wound down all the windows. The car had been baking in the sun all day; it was like sitting under a magnifying glass. He watched the world roll by for ten minutes, trying to ignore the butterflies in his stomach.

When he got back into the car, he put the radio on and turned it up so loud he couldn't hear himself singing. Heavy metal for once, which was usually forbidden in case the kids gave themselves whiplash copying his headbanging. Steve parked the car just outside the Lanson arena, home of Birmingham's rugby team. The casino was built in underneath it. It was huge, and felt more like a conference room which happened to have gaming tables in it. Steve heard the same playful tunes as he had from the Luton slot machines, but it was the clacking noise of chips being shuffled that drew him in.

Steve registered for the tournament, then walked over to the bar. He ordered a tequila and a pint of Jackpot ale, the Jacques-brand beer. He drank the tequila and almost a quarter of the ale before picking his pint up and turning away.

"Excuse me, sir! You need to pay for those." He turned back to see the bartender waiting, hand outstretched. Steve blushed, and reached for his wallet. *Don't get wrapped up in the situation*, he told himself. Someone chuckled to his right.

"Did you forget, or just feeling lucky?" The speaker was tall and slim, with a jawbone so sharp it could cut diamonds. He had ginger hair and a stubbly beard.

"Yeah, I'm a bit nervous, I haven't played for a while." Steve admitted.

"Ah, don't worry about it mate. I remember my first time playing in a casino, I could barely get off the toilet seat I was so nervous." He grinned and stuck out a hand. "My name's Grant."

Steve grasped Grant's hand and shook. "So, do you play much?"

"Oh yes mate, all the time. Been playing about nine years and love it. I'm playing as a pro, more because I don't have a job than because I'm really good, but I decided to have a chilled night tonight and come here." He paused. "I usually stream online if you ever watch Twitch?"

"I don't usually, but I'll check you out. I want to play more so it would be good to watch other people. What's your name online?" Steve asked.

"Dr Ibben." Grant replied.

An authoritative voice came over the loudspeaker. "Calling all players for the 7pm poker tournament! Your dealers are sat down ready and your seats are on the TV screens around the card room. We have a big crowd here tonight, so please can you take your seats and we will aim to get started on time."

"Well, good luck!" said Grant. Then he turned and became part of the crowd of people weaving among each other to find their seats. *I needed that,* thought Steve, who was now feeling considerably more relaxed.

Steve found his seat and settled himself before putting the glasses on. Then, pretending to adjust them, he pressed the frame down onto the bridge of his nose. The glasses flashed into life, the loading screen appearing across both lenses. He had been careful to make sure those were tinted, so nobody could see the images from the other side. The glasses were fully charged, and he had even remembered to put a powerpack in the car in case they needed an emergency top up. The *Loading...* message disappeared, and Steve watched the final players sit down. He had tested the glasses over and over in the mirror to make sure nobody could see what they could do. Even though he was sure they couldn't, Steve still shuddered with nerves. All fifty-two cards were laid on the table face-up, in order of value, and split into the four suits. For the first time Steve realised that he was sitting at one of the tables he had designed, and he took a moment to appreciate it before the tournament director, a bald middle-aged man standing by the registration desk, kicked things off.

"Welcome to Jacques Casino Birmingham! We're about to get our £30 Friday Frenzy underway. There are currently thirty entries; starting stacks are 18K and blinds will start at 25-50. Please remember the chips have no cash-equivalent value; some people have been chancing their arm at the cash desk over the last few days and we don't want to have to ban you. The blind levels will increase every twenty minutes. Remember, if you do bust, you can re-enter the tournament. Good luck, everyone. Dealers, shuffle up and deal."

The dealer swiped the cards up and started shuffling, and Steve's glasses went crazy trying to pick up the different patterns as the dealer washed the cards. There's the first thing I've learnt tonight, thought Steve. I can't watch the shuffle. He closed his eyes until the shuffling stopped, and opened them just as she began to deal. *Here we go!* Steve looked down. He had 6c 7c. Not a bad start, he thought, and threw in a raise to 150. He looked at the cards the player to his left, an old man with grey hair, was holding, and the glasses sprung up into life. 9d 2h, which were promptly thrown into the muck.

Steve felt a rush of adrenaline as the action folded around; the glasses registered each set of cards as he looked at them. His heart was almost bursting out of his chest and he had to clasp his hands hard to stop them trembling. The action folded around to the player in the dealer position, a large guy in his thirties with a Rick and Morty T-shirt which just covered the bulges of his body. He called with As Jd. The small blind folded and the big blind, a young Polish guy with a serious expression called with Kd 9d. The pot was 475 now, and Steve had the betting lead.

The flop was dealt: 6h 9c Qh. The big blind checked, and Steve bet 300. *Well, the big blind has paired his 9, so I'd expect him to call with that. If I bet big enough, I should be able to get rid of the fat guy.* Sure enough, the guy wearing the Rick and Morty t-shirt folded, and the polish guy called. The turn was Ad, which drew a look of disgust from the player who had just folded, but neither Steve nor the Polish player noticed. Steve was too busy counting out his chips to make a bet, eventually deciding to bet 800 into the 1075 pot. "Too expensive to see you turn over an ace and a queen!" he heard the Polish player say as he folded his cards. Steve did his best to suppress the grin on his face as he scooped the pot in. *I can't believe this is working.*

* * *

Steve decided to try and play decent hands, so he didn't wind people up by knocking them out with junk. He passed a few, then found himself with Kc Ks in the cutoff position, one place before the dealer. The action folded around to the player to his right, a man around the same age as Steve, who had Qc Jc and raised to 150. Steve decided to play it sly and called, throwing the same amount of chips in. Everyone else folded and it was just the two of them off to the flop. 10c 9h 7c,

Why didn't I re-raise? His opponent still had a worse hand, but any king, club or eight would give him a better one. *Time to make up for that,* thought Steve, facing a bet from his opponent of 300 into the 375 pot. He raised to 900 but his opponent called. Clearly, he had too much equity in the hand to fold. The 2c turn gave his opponent the flush, but he checked to Steve. Steve looked at the back of his cards. *I could make a better flush if there is another club on the river, I should check!*

The 3c on the river felt like a dream, which got even better when his opponent bet 2000. Steve reached for chips and raised to 6000, excited that he had managed to get to the river with the wining hand. The other player groaned.

"I'm not sure I can fold this; I've had you crushed all the way." He paused, then shrugged, threw another 4000 into the pot, and turned his Qc Jc over. Steve turned his pair of kings over proudly, and a chorus of 'Unlucky, mate,' rang out from the other players.

The Polish guy turned to Steve. "Bloody hell, mate, weren't you worried about an ace? I couldn't have raised that there."

"Nah, not really," Steve replied, suddenly unsure if he should feel confident or embarrassed about his play. His opponent could have had the Ac, which would have given him the best hand; but Steve could see that he hadn't and played accordingly. *Come on Steve, you need to think these things through a bit more, otherwise they'll work you out.* He started stacking his chips up, counting how many he had. *Twenty-six thousand! That must make me the chip leader.* Steve decided to sit back and wait for a decent hand before playing again, especially as he'd just been in the spotlight.

Half an hour passed, and Steve managed to keep his cool. Plenty of hands had been played and he was pretty sure his last, risky move had passed from the memory of the players. The player he had beaten hadn't taken losing well and punted the rest of his stack off shortly afterwards, receiving significantly less sympathy from the table for losing with third pair. Steve couldn't help but imagine a little black raincloud following the player around as he bleated about how unlucky he was. Eventually, Steve was dealt the 7h 7c in middle position. *Time to play*, he thought.

Steve raised to 600, three times the big blind. The action folded around to the player in the big blind, a squat man who reminded Steve of Vernon Dursley. He had As Ad, and of course he re-raised, making it 1800 to go. *What do I do now? I should have looked around at the other player's cards first* thought Steve. *Mind you, I could call and win a huge pot. If I hit a 7, I could take all of his chips.* He paused. *Feels like a bit of a gamble, though.* But the temptation was too strong. *Ah, fuck it!* he thought as he tossed the chips in, *I can always make it back in another hand if I don't hit.*

The flop came: Kc 7d 3h, *Boom!* The big blind bet 2000 and Steve decided to call, not wanting to raise any suspicions. The 9h turn changed nothing and the big blind bet again, making it 3500 to call. *OK, so I'm going to call again and then go all in on the River. Hopefully, he puts another bet out there as well; he'll feel committed to putting the rest in if he does.* Steve counted the chips out slowly, frowning, trying not to look too eager. He threw the chips in and the dealer burned the last card, the glasses picking up the 7s going into the muck. She turned over the river and time seemed to slow down as the Ah was laid beside the 9.

NOOOOO! That wasn't meant to happen! The other player counted out the rest of his stack before declaring 'All in' and staring at Steve. He'd got lucky; there were only two aces in the rest of the deck he could have hit to make a better three of a kind than Steve had. "Nice hand." Steve said disappointedly, and threw his cards into the muck. *That was a big loss,* he thought, as he looked down at his chips. *Back to 18K.*

Steve managed to win a few pots uncontested before the break and found himself back up to 27,000 as the tournament director announced the final hand before the break. Steve decided to fold his off-suit 9s 2d and head back to the bar. He reviewed his position as he strolled off. Two hours in, and so far, nobody had suspected he was cheating. Grant walked up to him just as he had ordered a Diet Coke, *I'd better not drink any more if I'm going to be up all night and drive two hours back to Hertford.* "Don't forget to pay this time!" he said, with a grin.

Steve laughed sharply "Do you want a drink?"

"Oh, cheers mate, I'll have a Jack Daniels and Coke if that's all right?" Steve nodded. "So how are you running?" Grant asked.

"Oh, you know. Won a few good pots here and there," Steve replied, doing his best to sound casual. "How about you?"

"Pretty good. I knocked a guy out just before the break, so I'm up to 40K. I haven't had many hands, but the ones I've had I've managed to get paid with. The knockout was pretty sweet, found myself on the right side of aces versus kings." Grant beamed.

"Ahh, nice one mate. Any decent players on your table?" Steve asked.

"Yeah, a few," Grant started pointing them out, oblivious to the fact some of the people from his table were standing next to him, trying to edge into his line of sight. They chatted for another five minutes before Grant excused himself to go the toilet. By the time he had returned the tournament director was calling the players to their seats and Steve was one of the first to get back. *Right,* he thought, taking his seat, *let's take this up a notch.*

Steve folded the next few hands until he found himself on the big blind with 7h 4h. It folded around to the small blind, a busty lady in her thirties wearing a low-cut top. who raised with As 5s to 1200. *I think I should call this,* he thought, tossing an additional 600 in.

The flop was dealt: Qh 7s 8c. *Brilliant, I've outflopped her and she doesn't have any draws to a flush or a straight.* The small blind bet 800. *Hmm. Not as much as I'd have liked her to put in, but I've only got to avoid an ace, so let's just call.* Steve sighed, and casually threw the chips in.

The dealer dealt the turn: 5h *Ooh, now that's an interesting card.* Steve's opponent bet 3000, seemingly more confident now she had a pair. Steve met her eyes. "How much have you got behind?" he asked casually.

"About 12K," she said, shrugging.

Steve decided to call, and the river was dealt: Ah. The perfect ace; a Trojan horse to trick his opponent into going broke. It gave her two pairs, but Steve had a disguised flush. His opponent bet 4500 and Steve didn't move a muscle. *Three, two, one...* As smoothly as he could, Steve declared "All in," pushing his chips over the line.

His opponent snap called, not realising the danger of the heart. She turned over her As 5s with confidence before Steve picked up each of his hole cards and turned them over. "Sorry love..." There were groans around the table at the runout of the cards in the middle.

"So sick!" the Polish guy shouted, his expression changed

from serious to one of sympathy.

"Damn, nice hand." she said, hardly able to get out of her seat. Eventually she stood and shook hands with Steve and a few of the other players on the table, before walking away into the flashing lights of the slot machines.

Once she had gone, Steve scooped in the chips. *I needed that,* he thought. He stacked them into nice neat piles and measured them up against each other, so he knew he had 10 chips in each stack. He'd found that was the easiest way to count his chips and it didn't take long for Steve to work out he was up to 35,000.

"OK ladies and gentlemen, we have just closed our re-entry period, which means the prize money is now on the screen," the tournament director announced. *£850 for first place, that's not a bad return on £30! Come on Steve, you can do this. Whatever the next hand is, I'll play.*

Steve idly ran his hand along the frame of his glasses as his cards were dealt. He peeked at the front of his cards though he already knew what he had; 9d 6s in the small blind.

There was limp from the under the gun player, the first player after the big blind, an elderly gentleman who had been limping all night with all sorts of playable hands including aces. This time, however, he had Jc 10s. It was folded around to Steve in the small blind who decided to limp as well. The big blind, a man in his fifties with a grey goatee, whom Steve had privately nicknamed Goatee Joe, decided to check. That surprised Steve as he had 9h 8h and a reasonably big stack. Not that he was complaining, since that meant it was easier to justify playing this type of hand.

The flop was 5c 4s Kh, which meant nobody had a hand. Steve decided to check, and Goatee Joe counted his chips out smoothly, betting 900. The old man folded, and Steve decided to call and see if he could get as many chips as possible. The turn was Ah, and Steve checked. Goatee Joe's shoulders seemed to have tightened, and he was aggressively clicking two chips together in his hands. He led again, betting 1800.

Steve realised he was slumping and sat up in his chair. He decided to stall over his decision a little and make Goatee Joe feel the pressure. He rested his head on his hand before counting out the chips and throwing them in with a splash.

The dealer swiped the chips into the pot and dealt the river: Ad. Steve had the worst hand, but Goatee Joe only had a 9 kicker to go with the pair of aces on the board, which wasn't great either. *He's got to bluff; it's the only way he can think he's going to win this hand. Shame I can see your cards, Goatee Joe!*

Steve decided to make a small bet. *He won't call, but Goatee Joe might raise.* He threw a single 1000 chip into the 7200 pot.

Goatee Joe leaned back in his chair and let out a gentle sigh. He looked down at his towers of chips and pulled one forwards. "Raise," he said in a gruff voice.

Steve stared at the chips in the middle, trying not to let himself smile. "I'm all in," Steve said, pushing a tower of his own over the line. Involuntarily he let out a little laugh, but Goatee Joe didn't react. He was clearly reeling; he simply couldn't call. Steve looked at the bet Goatee had in front of him; around 16000 chips. Goatee Joe had a quick last look at his cards, then threw them into the muck. Steve scooped in another monster pot, feeling electric.

* * *

Steve felt he had the full measure of how to use the glasses now, and continued to steal pots from players. As the other players were knocked out of the tournament, the tournament director would consolidate the players left, so that the tables were always full. Eventually, Steve found himself at the final table. Grant had also made it to the final table, and was sitting to Steve's right. Steve decided he wouldn't play against him until it was just the two of them, unless he got a premium hand.

"Bloody hell, you made it!" Grant exclaimed when they arrived.

"You sound surprised!"

"I am! No offence, it's just because you said you hadn't played for a while!"

"Ahh, good point. Must be re-beginner's luck!"

"Yeah, right!" They continued to chat between hands and the players began to fall away from the final table. Grant's phone flashed and Steve noticed two young girls on his background photo. "Are they your daughters?"

"Yeah, the elder is Lola, and the younger is Christina. Do you have any kids?"

"Yeah, two girls as well." Steve showed a picture of them to Grant. "Ellie and Fiona. I tried to get them into football, but it was no use, they weren't interested."

"Ha, me too! Who do you support?"

"For my sins, I support Watford."

"Ahh they're not doing too badly. Do you think they'll stay in the Premier League this year?"

"I'm not going to say yes until it happens. I'm *very* superstitious about football. How about you?"

"Nottingham Forest! We're pushing for promotion but don't think we'll make the automatic spots..." Grant tailed off as he raised to 10,000. Steve looked to his right, saw Grant had Ks

Kh, and quickly threw his 8d 3d into the muck. The action folded to the Polish guy Steve had played earlier, who silently pushed all of his chips forwards with 9h 9d. "Can I have a count please?" Grant asked the dealer.

"It's about 60,000." the Polish guy said, before the dealer had a chance to count the chips out.

"Yeah all right, I call," Grant said before turning his cards over. The board ran out Ah Qs 2c 3d 7d, and Grant won the pot with his pair of kings.

"Good game," said the Polish guy, shaking the hands of everyone at the table. They were down to four now, and Steve was the clear chip leader with just over a million chips. The rest of the players had less than 300,000.

"Are you married?" Steve asked Grant.

"Yeah, my wife's called Rebecca. We've been married for seven years and she works in logistics..." Grant's voice trailed off and he looked away. Eventually, there were just three of them left. Steve had the clear chip lead. Grant was in second and the third player a young guy called Simon with bad acne scars had just 60,000, which at the blind level of 5000/10,000 wasn't much at all. He shoved on Steve's big blind with Jc 3h, an easy call for Steve with Ac Js, even without the glasses, and then there were two. Steve looked at his watch. *3am. Fuck, I need to get home!* He thought quickly, then took a deep breath. "Listen, Grant, how about we do a deal?" he said. "First place is £850 and second is £600. I'll give you fifty and take £800 if you're willing to call it a night?"

Grant laughed. "Pfft! I could beat your ass all over the place heads up, pal!" Then he grinned. "I'll let you get away with giving me £75, since I saved you from the embarrassment of forgetting to pay for your drinks earlier!"

Steve laughed, although he wasn't sure if that was a joke. Then Grant held out a hand. "Alright, it's a deal! £75 it is!" Steve said, shaking Grant's hand. The tournament director gave them both prize tickets to exchange at the cashier, Grant getting £675 and Steve getting £775 in exchange for their tournament chips. They walked over together, the roulette and slot machines still busy with punters.

"You played well tonight, Steve," said Grant. "If you're up for it, we could swap numbers and maybe go to some tournaments together?"

"Do you know what, I'd be well up for that." Steve said, getting his phone out. They swapped numbers, before two cashiers became free. Steve watched the cashier count out his money in big red fifty-pound notes. He hadn't seen a fifty in a long time, and here were fifteen crisp ones about to become his. He picked the notes up, feeling the paper between his fingers before shoving them into a secret compartment in his wallet. *Holy shit, I could probably pay all my debt off doing this.* He could feel the weight of the bags under his eyes and remembered he had a two-hour drive to get home. "Grant, I'll text you tomorrow mate, I've got to run!" Steve shouted, and headed to his car.

The motorway was completely clear. Steve raced against the sat nav's predicted arrival time, singing along to Meatloaf. He beat the sat nav by five minutes, arriving back at 5:03 am. He went straight upstairs, set his alarm for 8am, and collapsed into bed. *This is going to be a tough shift,* he thought, and drifted into unconsciousness as the sun began to rise.

Chapter 6

G rant woke, the sun bursting through a gap in the curtains. The babysitter had stayed the night, and he was glad of the extra £25 from Steve, which he could give her as a tip. Rebecca was not in bed; she never had been one to sleep in. Grant swung his legs down and sat, rubbing his eyes. Then he looked at his phone. *Oh shit, it's two in the afternoon! I slept in again. Hang on, who's this?* Grant thought, opening a text from an unknown number.

Hi mate, it's Steve. Sorry I had to run, I live near London and needed to get home. Nice to meet you last night, and I'll let you know when I'm around for another game.

Huh, thought Grant, staring at the phone. *Weird he travelled all the way to the Midlands for a £30 tournament.* He texted Steve back: *Nice to meet you mate and well done on the win. Next time we meet up, the first round is on me.* He walked downstairs and into the kitchen, where a cup of coffee was waiting for him. His daughters were out in the garden playing and Rebecca was sitting at the table with her own coffee, chatting to Charlotte the babysitter. Charlotte was fifteen but wise beyond her years; she saved her babysitting money as a safety net for university. She also had a vocation for care and was very good at looking after Rebecca as well as the kids.

Rebecca had been ill, and they didn't know why. She fell over a lot, and found it hard to grip anything. They thought it was something not working in her brain, but Grant had tried to avoid the internet in case it diagnosed the symptoms as something more serious than it was. Rebecca was a fiery woman who didn't suffer fools gladly. She was also the operating director for a logistics company, and the definition of a self-made woman. She certainly didn't have any glass ceiling holding *her* back. It hurt Grant to see the strong woman he had married losing confidence. She'd stopped wanting to socialise with her friends as she was worried about embarrassing herself by falling over, or spilling a drink or some food down herself.

She was certainly different now from when Grant had first met her. They had been at a nightclub in Nottingham called Echo's, and he and his brother were out celebrating. The nightclub was a bit of a dive; the floors were sticky with spilt drinks and the place needed doing up, but the drinks were cheap, and the music was loud. He spotted her in the smoking area in a cream strap top and tight black leather trousers. She was sitting alone, and he wandered over. "Is it hot in here, or is that just you?"

"Ha! That's a terrible chat up line, but I haven't heard it before!"

"Sorry about that. My name's Grant."

"I'm Rebecca," she said, turning towards him as he sat down.

"So, you can't be here on your own, are you out with some friends?"

"Yeah, but they hate the smoking area. How about you, who are you here with?" she said, brushing her hair back behind her ear.

"I'm out with my brother, we're celebrating!"

"Oh yeah? Is it your birthday?"

"Yeah, it is! I'm twenty-three today!" Grant lied. He was twenty-three, but he'd just been released from prison for intent to supply drugs and they were celebrating his release. That was definitely something to tell her later. If at all.

"Well, happy birthday. We're out for my friend's hen do. I love her to pieces, but she's marrying a right shit. He cheats on her and she can't see that he doesn't love her. I think he proposed to get her to shut up moaning at him." She took a long drag on her cigarette and stubbed it out. "Do you want a cigarette?" She offered Grant one from her pack.

"Yeah, go on then!" Grant said, lighting one with her. "Listen, I'm not much of a dancer, but I'd love to get your number?"

"Blimey, you're forward! I don't just give it out to anyone, you know," she said playfully, swinging her hair out of her eyes like Marilyn Monroe.

A lightbulb suddenly went off in Grant's head. "Tell you what." He clapped his hands together. "I'll make a bet with you. If I win you have to go on a date with me, and if not, I'll leave you alone!"

"A *date* now, is it?" She raised an eyebrow. "All right then, what's the bet?" she said, grinning.

"I'm going to ask you five questions, and all you have to do is answer them incorrectly. If you answer one of them correctly then we go out!"

"Sounds easy enough. Come on then Grant, give me your best!" she said, leaning back in her chair ready for the game.

"All right, all right. A question … a question…"

"This is gonna be a long game if you can't think of any questions to ask me!" She laughed.

"OK, got one! What's your name?"

"Felicity Shagwell," she said, winking.

"*Felicity Shagwell?* Isn't that a character from Austin Powers?" he laughed, leaning forward in his chair.

"Ye... Nice try! I nearly fell for it" She laughed, bending forwards to knock the ash off her cigarette.

"OK, you've got the hang of this now. I'm going to try and make this a bit more difficult... What's the name of the nightclub?"

"San Marino's... I thought this was gonna be hard?"

"Damn, I thought I'd got you on that one... OK, a question... a question... Wait, how many questions have I asked?"

"I'm not falling for that one! You've asked 27!"

"Ahh dammit. Well that's sad for me, I guess I'm not going to be able to take the most stunning girl I've ever seen out on a date. Can't say I'm not gutted, but what can you do, eh? Have you played the game before or something?" Grant said with a glint in his eye.

"Never played it before, but I guess I just outsmarted you!"

"Actually, you didn't, because you just answered my fifth question!" Grant said, beaming.

"Oh, you cheeky bastard!" she said punching his arm. "That's so clever. Here you go then!"

They swapped numbers and went on a date, and then another, and ten years later they'd got married and had two daughters, Lola who was now ten, and Christina who was eight.

About half a year into dating, Grant came clean about the conviction. He'd found it hard to get a job, and as their relationship progressed, Rebecca had taken on the role of breadwinner. He had learned to play poker in prison, and found he had a talent for it. He studied it whilst being a stay-at-home dad, and played as a side hustle to Rebecca's income. Eventually, he started being able to contribute an extra couple of hundred pounds here or there. His overall confidence had grown enough that he felt comfortable starting a livestream of himself playing. Since Rebecca had become ill though, he had taken it even more seriously in case he needed to make it their main income.

Today they had an appointment with Dr Rashid, Rebecca's consultant at the hospital, to discuss test results. They had had a million appointments, where they were usually told about more tests that Rebecca needed, and Grant had no reason to think this would be any different. After a brief chat with Charlotte, he paid her £30 and added the extra £25 on top. He took a shower, got the kids into the car, and helped Rebecca in, carefully fastening her seatbelt after she had sworn at herself several times for not being able to do it. They drove to the hospital, taking it in turns to sing lines from 'Billie Jean'. Grant felt a trucker's tan developing on his right arm as they pulled into the car park. He paid the extortionate parking fee, and they walked to the neurology department.

* * *

"Rebecca Johnson?" a nurse with grey hair and a long nose shouted from the door.

"Yes, that's us." Rebecca called. "Come on, girls —"

"You don't need to bring your children. I'll ask one of the receptionists to keep an eye on them for you." the nurse said, walking to the desk. *That's unusual,* thought Grant. He suddenly felt nauseous, in just the same way he did when he had a monster poker hand, and in spite of it, found out that he was losing. He grabbed hold of Rebecca's hand as they walked through to the doctor's office.

Grant and Rebecca followed the nurse down the clinically white corridor to Dr Rashid's office, which was covered in certificates, and sat down, their faces showing their concern. The doctor was sat behind his desk riffling through a record on Rebecca. He had a kind face and spoke softly.

"We have the results back from your most recent scans," said the doctor, "and I have some news which will be hard to hear. You have motor neurone disease, which is a disease that affects nerves in your brain. Basically, they stop working. I'm afraid there is no cure, but with the right care, we can manage the disease well." He paused, scanning their stunned faces. "I'm sure you have many questions, so feel free to take your time to process this."

"Do I have long to live?" Rebecca blurted out.

Dr Rashid considered. "Usually people who get it live for between two to three years, but people can live for many years. Stephen Hawking is the obvious example."

"What symptoms will I develop?" Rebecca asked, tears gathering in the corners of her eyes. Grant looked away; he was finding it hard to compose himself. *Rebecca's my rock; how can this be happening?*

"Well, you are likely to find your grip getting worse, and feel weakness in your ankles and legs. Your speech may begin to slur. You might suffer from sudden weight loss and have difficulty swallowing. You might also find that you can't stop yourself laughing or crying in inappropriate situations." Dr Rashid's voice was monotone. Neither Grant nor Rebecca could find anything to say before Dr Rashid broke the silence again. "I'm going to prescribe you some Riluzole, which should help slow down the progression of the disease. I'll give you my card, and some leaflets in case you think of any questions after you have left here. I'd suggest we meet once per month until your condition deteriorates to the point where you feel it is having a significant impact on your standard of living. There is also a support group you can attend with the Motor Neurone Disease Association. There is a branch that covers Birmingham and Solihull; I'd recommend contacting them in a few days' time."

"Thank you, doctor." Grant stammered before both he and Rebecca rose to their feet. They walked out of the office and found Lola looking down at her mobile and Christina idly playing with toys that were clearly too young for her.

"Come on girls, time to go." Grant said sternly.

"Can I just finish this game before we go?" Lola asked.

"No, we need to go home now."

Lola scowled before jumping out of her seat and following her parents, head down looking at the screen. They drove home, Michael Jackson still playing on the stereo, but this time without anyone singing along. When they got home, Grant sent the kids went upstairs, and they were left alone. "It's so unfair!" Rebecca cried, burying her face in Grant's chest, and weeping into his T-shirt. "I want to give you years and years, not two or three! How are you going to afford to live, and look after the children, when I'm gone?"

"We'll make it work." Grant said, a firmness in his voice. Then he broke down too.

Chapter 7

Steve returned home from work a total zombie. He still couldn't believe his scheme had worked. He opened his wallet. The cash was there. It was real. *Should I tell Tanya?* he thought. *She might be mad that I gambled so soon after everything, but she might be happy that I can pay some of the debt off. Still, she might not let me do it again, in which case I can't use the glasses which seems like a waste. Particularly now I know they work. I think I'll keep this one a secret and use the money to get myself into some bigger entry tournaments.*

He looked at the cash in his wallet one last time before squirrelling the money away in an unused suitcase. Then he fired up his laptop and checked out upcoming tournaments. One caught his eye; a £220 entry tournament over two days at Jacques Nottingham, called the Summer Slam. It was the mini event; the main tournament was ten times as much, and Steve simply couldn't afford it. The tournament was in two weeks, which gave Steve some time to plan his approach. *Do I really want to go back there after everything that happened? It's unlikely that Alexander Jacques would be there, and even less likely that James will, so maybe it won't be so risky? Plus, it'd be good to get my revenge at the heart of the empire that screwed me. Fuck it, I'm going.* He texted Grant again: *Just spotted this tournament.*

Are you up for it? That accomplished, he finally succumbed to his fatigue.

A few days passed, and Steve wondered whether he would get a reply from Grant. It would be nice to go to tournaments and see a friendly face; it had certainly helped him calm his nerves the last time. Just as he had given up hope, his phone chimed. *Sorry mate, it's been a tough few days. I'm up for it, but you'll be playing for second place. I've got first locked up.* Steve laughed, then looked up and saw Tanya grinning at him. "What are you laughing at?" she asked.

Shit! Think of something, think of something! "Oh, just a stupid joke I've been sent by someone at work."

Tanya looked at him expectantly.

"Um…" Steve pretended to read from his phone. "Today my son asked me, 'Can I have a bookmark?', and I burst into tears. Eleven years old and he still doesn't know my name is Brian." *Bloody hell, where did that come from?* he asked himself.

"Hilarious," Tanya said, rolling her eyes.

* * *

The time dragged until the tournament. This time Steve had told Tanya that he was having a weekend away with 'the boys'. "Well, as long as they don't lead you astray you should go. With everything that's happened, it might do you some good to let your hair down a bit." *I love this woman so much*, Steve thought. She seemed genuinely happy that he was making new friends at work. Steve felt happy, too. He hadn't realised how much James had got him down, and was glad he was no longer in his life.

Steve drove up to Nottingham, relishing the time spent

driving with rock music up loud. He had used the suitcase he'd hidden the money in to pack his clothes and take it all with him. The last thing he wanted was Tanya finding some money hidden whilst he was away. Steve had agreed to meet Grant at the casino bar and walked quickly past the entrance to Alexander Jacques's office. *I haven't even thought about him since I booked this*, he warned himself. *That'll put you off your game.* As he approached the bar, Steve did a quick search for Jacques on Instagram and found a photo from the day before which showed him on a yacht with a plethora of scantily-clad girls. *Looks like he's on holiday again.*

"Hello, mate!" Grant shouted, interrupting Steve's thoughts. "I owe you a beer!" He slapped Steve on the back as he looked at the choice of drinks.

"I'll have a Peroni, please," said Steve.

"Two pints of Peroni and two tequila shots please, barkeep," Grant said, leaning on the bar. The bartender did not look impressed as he went about assembling the drinks.

"Woah, tequila as well?" Steve said, mirroring Grant's high spirits.

"Yeah, you made that a tradition at the last tournament!" Grant said, as the bartender put down their drinks, along with lemon wedges and salt. They each poured some salt into the L of their left hand, licked it, then picked up their shots. "Three, two, one!" cried Grant, and they both drank their tequila, then bit into a lemon wedge. The bitterness of the lemon tasted sweet against the harsh liquid. Steve shuddered as the burn spread down his throat and into his stomach, and Grant laughed at him.

"So, what's new, mate?" Steve asked.

"Not much, to be honest," said Grant. "I've been studying

the old poker pretty hard, so I'm feeling good and ready to kill! Not literally of course, just on the felt!" Grant laughed. "What about you?" Then he paused. "Oh yeah, I wanted to ask you something. Why do you travel all the way from London? Too many sharks down there?"

Steve considered agreeing. *But what if I want to play in London some time?* "I prefer the casinos up here. It gives me a chance to get away from it all for a little while." Steve replied, impressed by his new-found ability to lie.

"Ahh, fair enough mate." Grant seemed to have bought it. "Can't say I've ever been to any London casinos myself."

"Maybe we can go some time," said Steve. "Leicester Square's my favourite part of London. There's a wicked casino which used to be a theatre, and they have different tables on each floor. There's a bar on the balcony, and you can get a beer and watch people lose money at roulette without them knowing you're watching –"

He was interrupted by the loudspeaker. It was the tournament director. "Poker players for today's tournament, could you please take your seats as we are about to start." Steve felt a rush of adrenaline. *I can't wait for this.*

Steve's first hand was Ah Ad. *This is too easy,* he thought as he raised to 150. He was called by a guy wearing a red silk scarf, despite the summer weather, in the big blind who had As 10s. Steve thought he was dreaming, and then the flop came down: Ac 10h 10d. *Why can't this be happening later? How am I going to get all the chips in with the blinds this low?* His opponent checked before putting the scarf over his mouth. Steve bet high, counting what was in the pot and betting the same: 325. *This part the glasses can't help me with.* His opponent raised almost instantly, making the bet 1000.

Steve decided he had to play it fast, so raised again, making it 3000. His opponent frowned, the scarf not covering his forehead, then called. *Not bad, a bit of a starter before the main course.*

The turn was 2h, and the big blind checked. Steve bet 8000 and fixed his gaze on the cards in the middle. "Well, you've either got it or you haven't," the big blind said with a thick Italian accent, "I'm all in."

"Call." Steve couldn't get his chips in fast enough, and they both reached for their cards, ready to rake the pot in. They had both turned their cards face up before looking at what their opponent had. The whole table roared when the hands were revealed. "Oh my god, that's sick!" his opponent cried.

"Unlucky, mate." Steve said as his opponent stood up, still staring at the cards. He scooped the chips in using both arms to sweep them in front of him. *This must be what it's like to work on the roulette table.*

Steve was still stacking his chips when the next hand was dealt. He got 7h 2d before hearing someone at the table say, "I'm sorry, this card has been bent on the corner. Can we get some new ones?" Steve could see it was the Ad. *I must have bent it in my excitement.* The hands were folded around, and Steve decided he couldn't be bothered to try and bluff whilst he was still stacking his chips. The guy with the ace raised and everyone else folded. The dealer called for a new deck of cards, collecting the old ones in. Then he spread the new pack out face-up so the players could see none were missing. Steve finished stacking his chips up before looking down at the cards he had been dealt. The word ERROR flashed up in big red letters.

What the fuck? Steve looked at the other cards and the

ERROR message flashed up again and again. *Why can't I see the cards?*

The action folded around to Steve and he looked at his cards: Kh 10h. He was in middle position and knew he could afford to lose some chips. He raised to 150 and was called by four people. He lifted the glasses off his nose, wondering if he could switch them on and off again. ERROR flashed across his line of sight as he looked around. The flop came: Ks 10s 7d. Steve bet 300 and had two callers.

The turn was Jh and Steve bet again, this time betting 1000. Two more 1000 chips were thrown in by his opponents to match him. Steve raised an eyebrow, and felt a bead of sweat run down the side of his torso. He stared at both players. One was an elderly black man with grey and black hair and large black moustache, and the other a nerdy-looking blond with a crooked nose. Both did their best not to make eye contact with Steve. *Damn, what the hell are you calling me with!*

The river was the 6h and Steve hesitated, possibilities racing through his mind. *What if one of them has king jack, or a set? Maybe they called with ace queen, or queen nine, and got there on the turn, and they're trapping me? A flush is the obvious missed draw, but could they both have a flush draw? I must bet; I've got a solid two pairs and they might fold.*

Steve bet 2500 into the 4500 pot. The moustachioed man called 2500 but Steve heard the word he had been dreading. "Raise," the crooked-nosed player said, before making it 15000 to go. *Oh, that is a massive over-bet. Maybe he's trying to scare us both off with a missed flush draw? Maybe he has a six and a seven and made two pairs on the end? POKER IS SO HARD.*

Someone laughed, and Steve realised he had said the last sentence out loud. He was still running through all the hands his opponents could have when someone shouted "Clock." The tournament director was called over by the dealer. "The clock has been called on this gentleman," the dealer explained.

"And has the player had enough time to act?" The dealer nodded his head. "OK sir, you have a minute to act from now. I will count down the last ten seconds." The time flew and he heard the tournament director counting down from ten. He tossed a chip in, indicating a call before the other player folded. The raiser flipped over the 8s 9s for a turned straight. "Nice hand." Steve said, annoyed the player hadn't raised their straight on the fourth community card.

Steve made it through to the break, but not without losing all the chips he had won in his first hand, and half of his 30,000 starting stack. He spotted Grant walking across the room with what could only be described as swagger. "How are you getting on, pal?" he asked as he approached.

"Absolutely horrendous to be honest," said Steve. "I won a massive pot at the start and then my chip stack has fallen faster than a whore's drawers. How about you?"

"Killing it, mate," said Grant, smiling. "I knew studying would help. I've been bluffing in the right places and getting value from all the suckers on my table. Reckon I'm on about 75K."

"Glad you're doing well mate. You don't fancy doing a swap, do you?" Steve grinned to show he didn't mean it.

"Tell you what, let's do a deal. If I win any cash, I'll give you 10%, and you do the same?"

"Really? Even though you know I'm basically out?"

"Of course, Steve. You gave me a bit extra last time, and you didn't have to." Grant said, sticking his hand out. Steve gripped it and shook firmly. "Still your round though!" Grant laughed.

After Steve finished his drink, he excused himself to go to the bathroom. He *had* to check the glasses. He locked himself in a cubicle, took the glasses off, and examined them minutely. *There's no damage to the frames ... the battery is fully charged...* He looked at the switch and flicked it to infrared-only. *He couldn't have ... could he?*

* * *

Steve sat down at the table and stared at the top card. *He has. He's changed the patterns.* He was looking at cards he hadn't designed and that he couldn't read. *He must have hired someone who worked out how to do it.* Steve suddenly became aware that the table was full, and the dealer was shuffling the cards. He looked down at his chips. 15000, not that much. Steve felt defeated. He had already lost his buy-in, and now his chance to use the glasses was slipping away. *I need to analyse the patterns, get some of the cards.* Steve looked at his hole cards, 6d Ks. *Fold.* He looked up at the ceiling and saw a million black domes staring back down at him. *Well, I can't just swipe them. Where do they even keep the spares?* He looked around for inspiration, but found none.

Another set of cards was dealt to him, and Steve was looking at 3c 3h. The action was on the moustachioed player who was hesitating about what decision to make. With all eyes on the other player, Steve took his opportunity. Covering one hand with the other, he dug his nail as hard as he could into the top of one of the cards. When the action came round to him, he said, "I'll fold, but this card has a mark on it." Steve showed the card to the dealer, who pulled it to the centre to check after the hand had played out. Two minutes later, he was holding the card up to the light. "This doesn't seem right…" the dealer said, almost to himself. "Floor on table 22," he shouted, before pursing his lips together to make a kissing sound to attract attention of the tournament director.

The tournament director came to the table, his gut gently brushing the backs of the players' chairs as he passed. The dealer spoke in a hushed voice before passing the card over. Steve watched; his breath held. The tournament director held the card up to the light in the same way the dealer had, the dealer murmuring in his ear. Suddenly the tournament director's gaze fixed on Steve, whose heart skipped a beat. *Oh my God oh my God oh my God, they know it was me. I'm going to get caught.*

"Cards on table 22!" the tournament director barked. Behind the registration desk a dealer ducked before bringing over a new set of cards. "This new brand of cards is rubbish," the dealer said under his breath to his manager. "They mark really easily. Why can't we go back to the old KEM cards?" Steve heaved an involuntary sigh of relief, which drew a few odd looks from the players around him.

"Since when have the guys at the top ever tried any of the new stuff they bring in?" the tournament director replied, sour-faced. The new deck was spread face-up on the table, and they played on.

Steve was in the big blind and looked down at Ac Kd. It folded around to the button who raised to 3000. The small blind folded, and Steve declared he was all in before being snap-called by the button, who had Ad As. *I really miss seeing people's cards,* Steve thought. The flop, turn, and river didn't help, and Steve was eliminated from the tournament.

He walked over to the bar and ordered a Diet Pepsi. *How the hell am I going to get hold of these new cards? How many different packs do they have?* Then a new thought occurred to him. *Maybe I could ask if me and a friend could borrow some cards to play something?* Steve felt as if he had nothing to lose, so strolled over to the registration desk as casually as he could. Despite his best efforts, though, his legs stiffened, and he couldn't make eye contact when he reached the desk. He cleared his throat. "Hey mate, any chance me and a friend could borrow some cards to play a quick game?" Steve said, his voice wavering.

The man behind the desk looked up from his phone, his striking blonde hair reflecting the lights. "Sorry mate, we can't lend any cards out. Company policy. What did you want to play, anyway?"

Taken unawares, Steve blurted out "Um, snap?" He regretted it immediately as the dealer raised an eyebrow.

"Well, maybe you could try blackjack instead?" Steve walked dejectedly back to the bar. *Come on Steve, think of something.* He sipped his drink, watching the world carry on around him. He looked at his watch. 9:25pm and he was already out.

Then a man in casino uniform walked up to the bar. "Hi, I'm Jeff. I'm starting work here today?" he said nervously.

"You're kidding!" the bartender replied, staring at him. "Why does nobody communicate in this place?" Steve took a deep draught of his drink. Something had turned up. But he was going to need a suit, a briefcase, some decks of cards, a wig, and a heck of a lot of luck.

* * *

Steve found Grant behind a huge pile of chips. He waited for a break in the play before he called over to Grant. "I'm going to head back to the hotel, mate. I'm not feeling it tonight. I'll come back tomorrow and ship something instead. If your arms aren't too tired scooping in all those chips, we can grab a beer tomorrow afternoon, maybe?" Then Steve drove back to his hotel room and fired up his laptop. As it was loading, he noticed a carving in the desk his laptop was on. 'Gaz woz 'ere 2018' *I hope you had a better time than me, Gaz,* thought Steve.

The room was badly in need of redecoration. The walls were a faded shade of mustard yellow, and were scuffed and marked. The shower was in the corner, with a curtain that barely stopped the water getting into the bedroom carpet. It had started to get black with mildew around the bottom. The double bed had clean sheets on it, but other than that and the low price, there wasn't much positive to say about the place.

Steve browsed the internet and found a Primark store where he knew he'd be able to get a cheap suit. Luckily, there was a bag shop nearby where he could get the briefcase, and he found a games shop which he was certain would sell some high-quality cards. He also searched for the highest rated wig shop he could find. He wrote it all down in a notepad and spread the sheets of paper out across the desk. *This is like being a detective who's trying to solve a case he couldn't handle twenty years ago... Are you really going to do this?* A pang of nerves hit his stomach and grew within his belly.

Steve got ready for bed and lay there with the lights switched off, staring at the ceiling. Occasionally car headlights would illuminate the room, waking him from the light sleep he'd found it hard to find. At around two am, the Friday night revellers made their way home, shouting abuse at one another. Steve stared at the ceiling until the sun began to rise.

Chapter 8

The sound of ducks quacking filled Steve's hotel room, his alarm indicating it was 7.30 am. He should have felt tired, but the adrenaline coursing through his body meant he was wide awake. He had a shower before leaping over the patch of wet carpet and getting dressed. He walked into town, bought himself a bacon sandwich and a coffee and reviewed his plan.

Should I use my card? if I get caught, they could trace my transactions. I could use the extra cash I brought up with me. Oh, I can't be arsed to walk back to the hotel, I'll put it back in my account later. He withdrew £300 from his account, wincing at the dent he'd made in his balance. *I hope this will be enough.* Finding the suit was easy; he picked the first one he could find that fit him. The briefcase was also easier than he'd expected, and he picked up one that would hold the decks of cards he would need. As he ticked everything off the list, he felt some of the weight lifting from his shoulders. The plan was coming together.

Steve walked over to the board-game store as the Saturday shoppers were starting to head out in their droves. *At least I'm hiding in plain sight.* He walked into the store, which was already heaving. Steve walked up to the counter, behind which stood a man with a large black beard and long hair.

"What's going on in here today? It's busy!" he said.

"Yeah, we have a *Magic, The Gathering* tournament going on today. Do you play?"

"I'll be honest, I've never heard of it."

"Here, I'll give you this starter guide. It's great fun. Anyway, what can I help you with?"

"I'm looking for some packs of KEM brand playing cards. Do you have any?"

"Sure, how many do you need?"

"About twenty packs."

The shopkeeper laughed. "Sorry pal, we wouldn't order that many as part of a normal stocktake." He tapped at his terminal and frowned. "We've got 4 decks in stock. I can give you another brand if you'd like?" *This is going to be a problem. The casino will want high quality cards... But maybe I can get away with it. I only need them to believe they're all KEM for a few moments.*

"All right mate, can you make up the rest with cards that have a similar packet?"

The shopkeeper frowned through the mass of hair. "I'll see what I can do." He walked into a stockroom behind the counter and Steve looked around whilst he waited. *I could run a business like this...* The man returned with a box full of playing cards. "These were the closest I could get." *At least the packs are the same colour,* Steve thought as he looked into the box full of white packs of playing cards.

"Why do you need them to be the same-coloured packets?" The shop assistant frowned.

"They're a prop for a film set." *There's that easy lying again...*

"Oh, that's cool. What's it going to be called?"

"The Card Shark." *Where is this all coming from?*

"Cool, is anyone famous going to be in it?"

"Actually yeah, Bradley Wiggins is in it." *NO, NO, NO...*

"Bradley Wiggins? You mean the cyclist?"

"Yup," Steve said before holding his breath.

"Huh, weird. I never saw him as an actor."

"Yeah, me neither, but there you go. How much is that?"

"£120 please." Steve did his best to hide his discomfort at the amount of money he was handing over. After he'd paid, he made a quick exit, walking back to his car to put his shopping in the boot. He leaned on the parcel shelf and retched, before regaining his composure. Then he looked in his wallet. He had £50 left. He set off to the wig shop and found a blonde wig that just about fit over his head. He bought it and walked back to the car. *OK, you've had your moment of idiocy for today. Time to switch it on now.* Steve drove to the Jacques Casino Nottingham, stopping in a car park halfway to change into his disguise.

* * *

Steve got out of the car and walked to the reception, dressed in the suit and wig, and carrying a full briefcase. Behind the desk was a man with grey hair and huge bags under his eyes. He looked as if he'd been there all night. "Hi," said Steve briskly. "I'm from Baldwin and Ash Gaming Tables and I have an appointment with the card room."

"No problem, I'll give them a quick ring and let them know you're here." Steve's leg jiggled in anticipation as the receptionist dialled. "What's your name?"

"James Baldwin." Steve replied. Another haggard man came to reception, and Steve couldn't concentrate on anything other than his teeth, which were too large for his mouth and impossibly white.

"James, good to meet you," he said, offering a hand. "My name is Ron, and I'm the card room manager. We weren't expecting you today?"

"We've had some complaints from other card room managers that the cards have been marking easily, so I've come down to see if you've had the same problems. Head Office were meant to let you know that I was coming," Steve said, not breaking eye contact.

"Oh, that lot never tell us anything, they're utterly useless." Ron snapped. "Listen, have you got any ID on you?"

"I'll be honest," said Steve, "I bought a coffee at a service station on the way up here and left my wallet on the counter when I picked the coffee up. I'm such a clumsy bugger. I didn't even realise until I'd got here and tried to check into the hotel. If you like, though, I've got Alexander Jacques's number in my phone here. I can give him a quick ring and he'll vouch for me." He held up his phone, then looked at his watch. "I wonder what time it is in the Bahamas?" he said, as he pretended to look through his contacts.

"No, don't ring him!" cried Ron. "I'll take you through." He set off as if Alexander Jacques himself was on his tail, and Steve followed, smiling to himself.

Ron took Steve to the poker room, which was almost empty except for one table which had five people playing cash. He walked over to the registration desk before motioning Steve to follow in behind, before bending down and opening a safe. Steve surveyed the stacks of bank notes, chips, and decks of cards, and it occurred to him that he must be the first person ever to rob a casino safe and leave all the money. "These ones in the cardboard box are the marked ones," said Ron. "We haven't had a chance to cut the corners off yet, but they're duds." Ron pulled some decks out and handed them to Steve.

"I'm going to need to take all of these," said Steve, unlocking his briefcase so that he could fill it with the marked decks of cards. The cards he'd bought from the shop stuck out from the top of a pocket in the briefcase. "I've brought you some replacement KEM decks; they won't register on the cameras, but they should last a bit longer. We'll sort out some proper replacement ones, and Head Office will send them over as soon as they can." he smiled.

"Thanks," said Ron, "but we're on strict orders only to use the ones that can be read. I'm surprised none of the other managers mentioned that." He eyed Steve.

"To be honest, Ron, this is the first time I've offered them out," Steve replied. "By the way, how many of the new patterns have you got in circulation?" *I'm going to look stupid if there's only one,* he thought.

"Oh, we've got all eight of them going round," Ron replied. *Holy shit! Eight patterns?* thought Steve. *How did they churn them out so quickly?* He scratched his head, thinking, before realising that the motion of his hand was disturbing his wig. He saw Ron frowning, and stopped at once.

"Thanks for your help, Ron. I'll get over to the other casinos to pick theirs up, then we can send them back to the supplier and tell them to sort it out. See you soon." Feeling his face flush with embarrassment, Steve made for the exit.

"James, wait there one minute," said Ron's voice, behind him. "James, stop." Steve picked his pace up, not daring to look back. "James, hang on one second." Steve heard Ron's footsteps quicken behind him, then a hand touched his shoulder. *Fuck, I'm busted.* Steve turned around to see Ron holding out a deck of cards. "You dropped these on the floor, mate." Ron said, slapping the deck into Steve's hand.

* * *

Steve got into his car and drove off in silence, not even putting the radio on. He pulled into the same car park he'd changed in before, and changed back into his normal clothes before continuing his journey. He parked the car, and the engine shuddered to a halt. Steve roared, the sound coming from deep in his gut, before beeping his car horn in celebration. He'd stolen from a casino safe and got away with it! Then he calmly got out of his car and walked back to his hotel room and emptied the marked decks onto the bed.

Steve turned his laptop on, and plugged the glasses into it. He switched them to infrared and opened the first deck. He sorted the cards consecutively, first by suit and then by value. Then he placed them face down, got a beer from the minibar, and looked at the As through the glasses. They picked up on the new pattern on the back of the cards, and the software on his laptop calibrated the pattern until it had matched it 100%, making a satisfactory *beep* when it was finished. The new pattern was more angular and far cruder than the curvy lines he had initially designed around the visible artwork on the back of the card. *Typical James laziness,* Steve thought. *Can't be arsed to change the artwork, just draws over the top of it.*

Steve continued running through the deck. It was a laborious process, but Steve felt the thrill of espionage. This was the closest he would ever get to being James Bond. He helped himself to a second beer from the minibar. Eventually, Steve had scanned through all the decks he'd got from Ron.

Unfortunately, that was only six decks out of the eight that were running. But that meant he'd got three-quarters of the cards in use; he could always request a new deck if he got one the glasses couldn't read. He stretched, then looked at his phone. The time had flown by. It was three in the afternoon and he had four missed calls and two voicemails from Grant. *We were meant to go for a beer, they must have started by now.*

In anticipation of a few more beers at the casino, Steve ordered a cab there. He strolled into the card room and saw that Grant was on a table surrounded by cameras and stage lights. *This is new,* thought Steve. *I'm glad I'm not in.* He tried to imagine the complications of using his glasses to win hands, when everyone could see he always made the right decision. He caught Grant's eye, and Grant nodded at him as if to say *it's all under control, mate.* "Do you want a beer?" Steve shouted, and Grant gave him a thumbs-up. *He's a bit quiet. Maybe he's nervous about being on the TV table.*

Steve wandered to the bar and ordered two beers and two tequilas. Out of the corner of his eye he saw Ron going about his business, instructing dealers where to go, and giving rulings when a table needed a tournament director's input. Steve did his best to try and hide his face. He walked back to the table with the drinks and railed his friend. Steve was pleased to see his glasses were picking the cards up again, and he noticed Grant was playing a little tighter today than the bouncy image he had projected yesterday. He looked at the stacks and calculated that Grant was on about 750K, which was just above the average. The blinds were 10K/5K with a 10K Big Blind ante. *Pretty healthy. Don't do anything stupid, mate, and you should be looking good for the final table.* There were seventy players left, and thirty-two would win prize money.

Steve wandered over to the registration desk and signed up for the side tournament, a £60 entry tournament with a £6000 guarantee. He sat down at the table and recognised a few of the players from the tournament the day before. He frowned, trying to remember how they had played, before realising that it didn't matter now, since he could see what cards they had.

* * *

Once the cards started flying, Steve felt his mojo come back. He found it easy picking up chips, turning his 15K starting stack into 48K by the break. He had been trying out a new strategy, aiming never to go to showdown, where the players would get to see his hole cards, unless he had the winning hand and the cards were respectable. It was fine to show As Qs as a winning hand, for example, but showing down with something like Kd 2c would make the other players at his table think of him as a fish; not a good reputation to get so early on in the tournament. If they thought he was a bad player, it might be harder for him to bluff them. Occasionally he gave a few chips back to the other players, but never anything that was hugely damaging. He might call a bet when he had a flush draw, and he knew he had the worst hand, but the turn or river could bring the fifth card of the same suit. Sometimes he got there, sometimes he didn't, but as long as it wasn't too expensive, he didn't mind.

Steve kept his eye on the live stream, to see how Grant was doing. The stream had a thirty-minute delay on it to prevent anyone cheating. Unfortunately, the breaks for the tournaments weren't synchronised, so, after playing for two hours on his own table, Steve went to watch his friend but couldn't really talk to him. Grant's face wore a look of deep concentration, and his chip stack was now slightly lower than average. He didn't even notice Steve. There were thirty-five players left, meaning only three players would be knocked out without any prize.

"Seat table three!" Steve turned to see someone getting up from the table, his face thunder. He just caught a glimpse the cards before the dealer scooped them up. It looked like the busted player had had his pocket aces cracked by pocket kings, with the kings making three of a kind on the river. *No wonder he's pissed off, there were only two cards in the whole deck he could lose to.*

Suddenly Ron's voice blasted out through the speakers. "All right players, we are one away from the prize money, so we are going to play hand for hand. Dealers, please deal one hand only; we will deal the next hand once all hands on each table have been completed. Players, if there is an all-in and a call, please don't turn your cards over until you are given the go-ahead. OK, dealers, please deal the next hand."

Steve watched Grant's table; there were two short stacks immediately to Grant's right. Grant was in the big blind, but everyone folded to him, meaning he won the pot uncontested. "Ah, look at this rubbish!" he exclaimed, turning over Ah Ad. Steve hung around Grant's table, careful to avoid Ron's eye-line, and worked out that Grant had around 25 big blinds; not a short stack, but by no means comfortable. He watched another hand go uncontested, Grant folding the small blind. For the next hand, he found himself on the button and the action folded around to him. He looked to his left and realised that both the players left to act had fewer chips than he did. "I'm all in," he announced firmly, pushing his chips forwards.

The small blind folded. The big blind, the black-moustachioed man, looked at his cards, sighed and pushed his chips forward to indicate a call. The big blind's stack was about half the size of Grant's. Grant couldn't be knocked out, but he would be in trouble if he lost.

Again, Ron strode around, Steve began mirroring his movements in the knowledge he'd come to the TV table. Ron checked all the hands had finished before asking the players to turn their cards over. Grant had Ah Jd and his opponent had Ac Kc. Grant was dominated and had only three jacks he could hit to win. "OK, dealer, please deal the flop."

The flop was dealt: 5d 7c Jh. His opponent stood up from his chair, shouting "Come on dealer, one time!" Steve had heard people call 'one time' at tournaments before, usually when they were all in and losing, but he was uncharacteristically superstitious about saying it. *You only get one 'one time', and the only occasion I'll say that is if I'm at the final table of the World Championship of Poker, or I need a card because it's going to be life-changing. The poker gods can be fickle,* he thought.

"Dealer, the turn, please," Ron called into the microphone. The dealer turned over the Kd; now Grant's opponent had the higher pair.

"Yes, that's what I'm talking about!" he shouted before high-fiving one of his friends. *Too soon,* thought Steve. *Still two jacks out there.*

"Ok, so we will remain hand for hand unless we see a jack on the river. Dealer, please can you deal the final card." The dealer burned a card and turned over the Js. "We have lost our final player," said Ron. "Congratulations, everyone, you're all now in the money!"

The four tables playing burst into applause, with some

players cheering. Normally Steve felt sorry for the person who was applauded as the final loser, but after the man's reaction on the turn, Steve couldn't help but feel he deserved it. He gave Grant a thumbs-up, and saw him puff out his cheeks in relief.

* * *

Steve went back to his table and the time flew. As he approached the bubble in his own tournament, the final table was beginning to start in Grant's. Grant had sent him a text: *Reckon I'm 8th in chips, 9 left. If I can double up, I'm in with a shot of winning.* First place was a cool £12,000, but there was a long way to go till there. If Grant were knocked out now, he'd be looking at £750. It would still be a decent prize, but it would be hard not to feel disappointed for him.

Before he knew it, the bubble in his own tournament burst and Steve didn't get a chance to really take advantage. That didn't matter too much, though; now the bubble had burst, people who didn't have many chips, and were hanging on to get into the money, started shoving them all in. Steve won a 40K all in with 6d 6s versus 4d 4s, and in the next hand someone shoved 50K with 7s 7h versus his Ah Qc. There was roughly a fifty-fifty chance he would win, and he didn't mind taking that type of gamble when he had a lot of chips behind him. The board ran out 6c 9d 3h Qd 3s, and Steve scooped his chips in with a turned pair of queens, beating the pocket sevens.

Steve glanced over at the feature table. There were still nine players sitting down. Steve decided to let someone else win a few hands and see how Grant was doing. As he approached the railings which stopped people getting into camera-shot he heard Grant say, "All in". His opponent had a mountain of chips in front of him and Steve could see he was the chip leader. He had a thick ponytail, which brushed the back of his neck as he called, and they turned their cards over. The flop had already been dealt: Ac 7s 9s in the middle of the table. Grant had Ad Ah for three of a kind, and his opponent had 8s 10s. Technically that meant he had eight high, but a lot of cards could give him a better hand than Grant's three of a kind. In fact, Steve wasn't exactly sure who was most likely to win. He tried to calculate some rough probabilities, but he wasn't fast enough to do it before the dealer dealt the turn, 3h. *That's safe, just avoid a six, a jack or a spade!* The dealer burned a card and turned over the As.

The chip leader bounced out of his chair to celebrate, then realised he'd lost. He'd made his flush, but the ace gave Grant four of a kind. "Steve, you're my good luck charm!" said Grant, beaming. "Every time you come over; I seem to win."

"Don't jinx it!" Steve replied, smiling. Grant had needed that win. He was now up to around forty big blinds and Steve reckoned he was fourth or fifth in chips. In the very next hand, the shortest stack on the table busted, losing with Ah 4h versus the Ad Kd of the chip leader. *Eight left,* thought Steve, clenching his fists. *Come on Grant, you can win this.* Steve walked back over to his table, having left his stack unattended to watch Grant for longer than he'd planned. *I wish I could watch Grant, it's exciting! Mind you, I don't think Grant will pay for my wig and suit!* A few players had been knocked out, and there seemed to be one recipient of all the chips: a tall wiry man sitting opposite the dealer.

"You've been winning whilst I've been away, then?" Steve said, with a smile. The man looked daggers at Steve, grunted in acknowledgement, then fixed his eyes back on the current hand. *Fucking hell, what an arsehole!* thought Steve. *If he's so grumpy playing poker, I suppose I should put him out of his misery.*

In the next hand, Steve was dealt 7s 2c *Ha! What better hand to start with than the worst in poker?* Steve raised to 15K. *Bloody hell, the blinds have gone up,* he thought, looking at the large screen on the wall. The wiry man called with 8h 8d and the big blind also called with Ah 10s. *Hmm, I didn't really want the big blind in, that's another person I need to bluff out of the pot.*

The flop was dealt: 6c 7c 2s *Holy shit, I've got two pairs!* The big blind checked, and Steve bet 30K into the 52.5K pot. The wiry man pondered, then raised to 75K. The big blind folded, and the action was back on Steve. *I don't really want to show down this hand, but I can't fold.* He threw an extra 45K out and the dealer scooped the chips in. Steve looked down at his stack. He had around 300K left, and the wiry man had about 250K. The pot was big already at 202K, and Steve decided this was where the hand would stop. He declared "All in" on the 3s turn, and the wiry man hesitated about his decision. Steve watched as he separated his chips into two piles, then clumsily attempted to merge the two stacks into one. He picked two of his chips up, one in each hand, and started clicking them against each other as though trying to light a fire with two stones. Then a chip slipped out of his hand and over the line. The dealer saw the chip cross the line and said, "Call, showdown please," in a thick Italian accent. *I really didn't want to show this hand down,* thought Steve. *it's going to ruin my image.* But he'd been asked to show down, so he reluctantly turned his cards face up.

"No, no, I didn't mean to do that," the wiry man protested angrily. Then he glanced at Steve's cards and went almost purple in the face. "Why are you playing hands like that, you stupid idiot? Are you slow in the head?"

Steve couldn't think of anything witty to say in response. "Oh… fuck off, you grumpy bastard." The dealer had been trying to beckon the floorman to the table, but the players had made enough noise to summon him.

"Can you tell me what happened?" the floorman asked. Steve was happy to see it wasn't Ron but one of his team providing the ruling.

"This gentleman went all in, and one of this gentleman's chips was in after that," said the dealer, pointing to each player in turn. "*He* says it was an accident, but I don't know if he's saying that now he's seen this man's cards."

"I didn't mean to call," whined the wiry man. "The chip went across accidentally, then after I protested, he called me a grumpy bastard!" He pointed at Steve accusingly.

"You only said that *after* you saw my hand." Steve replied, getting his two cents in.

"Right, this is what's gonna happen," the floorman said, as if telling off a pair of children. "As this man's cards are exposed and a chip has crossed the line, it has to be considered as a call, otherwise you will have an unfair advantage when making your decision. The man with the exposed hand will get a three-hand penalty after this hand has finished for swearing at another player. Dealer, please deal the river."

The river was dealt — the As — and the wiry man was out of the tournament with a pair of eights versus Steve's two pair, sevens and twos. He stood up and walked towards Steve, then shouted, loud enough for everyone in the card room to hear, "How can you raise with seven two? I hope you're happy, you fucking idiot. Next time, read a book before you come and play."

Steve half-rose. "Listen mate, I think you should just leave. You need to calm down —"

"I'll show you calm down," the man spat. He threw a punch which caught Steve on the cheekbone and knocked him flying, his glasses skittering across the floor.

Steve opened his eyes to find himself surrounded by people. He looked for the wiry man and saw him being manhandled by the security team towards a staff-only door. *Where are my glasses?* Steve thought, panicking. He stood up, aided by some of the players gathered around him. Steve frantically looked around for the glasses before spotting one of the floormen crouched down by a seat at one of the other tables, and the glasses on the floor beside him. He held them out with a smile, and the first thing Steve noticed were his impossibly white teeth. Ron did a double take. "Are you alright?" he asked, passing the glasses over to Steve. "James Baldwin, right?"

Steve took the glasses quickly and put them back on. "Thanks, and no, my name is Steve," he said in a deep voice.

"You're the spitting image of someone I met this morning," said Ron, with less certainty. "Do you have a brother called James?"

"Not that I know of. Maybe my dad's been a busy man!" Steve said, with what he hoped was an un-James-like grin. The *Loading...* message appeared before his eyes *SHIT! Can he see this?*

"Do you need any first aid?" Ron asked, seemingly oblivious to the technology in front of him. Steve touched the side of his face, but found no blood, just a sore patch. *This is bad, this is really, really bad.* "I think I'll be all right."

"Show's over!" Ron shouted. "Back to your seats, everyone."

The crowd dispersed, and Steve retook his seat at the table.

"Sorry about that," he said, to the table in general, then settled back to watch. He was quite shaken, and glad to have a three-hand penalty to gather his thoughts.

A hand rested firmly on his shoulder. "Are you OK, Rocky?" Grant said.

Steve chuckled. "Yes thanks, mate. I've never actually been punched before, so that's a new experience."

"Well, next time you might even get a chance to throw one back!" Grant grinned. "As soon as I saw what was happening, I was out of my seat, but the security team beat me to it. I can't believe he punched you when you were getting up, that's not even a fair fight!"

"Lots of things aren't fair in the world," Steve replied.

"Yeah, that's true." Grant said, looking rather lost, and Steve felt bad for distracting him from the main business.

"How are you getting on in the tournament?" he asked.

"Good!" Grant exclaimed, returning to the present. "I'm third in chips and there's six of us left."

"Bloody hell, it wasn't just me getting knocked out then! I didn't see anyone standing up from the table."

"That fella with the ponytail is on a tear. Reckon it'll be me and him heads up, and then I can kick his ass!"

"Well, I'll be up for seeing that. Good luck, mate."

Grant raised a hand. "Catch you in a bit," he said, walking back to his seat.

Steve had one more hand to sit out, but decided only to play broadly respectable hands after the reaction his 7-2 had got. *Keep a low profile, you don't need any more attention.* He didn't get a chance to be dealt another hand on that table, though, as one of the players busted with Ad Ks against the Qs Qc of an opponent who covered him by 1000 chips.

They broke the table to bring the final nine together, and Steve felt excitement unsettle his stomach. The top prize in his tournament was £1500, which would be a good win and a decent amount of money to reinvest. He could even start paying of some of his debt. At any rate, he needed to get a few places higher. If he busted now, he'd win £180, which wouldn't even cover his new suit and wig. Steve closed his eyes and thought of his daughters. *OK. Game face.*

* * *

An hour and a half passed, and Steve found himself heads-up against a player who had continually gone all in with the worst hand and won. Steve hadn't played very much following his altercation, and had a lower stack now than when he sat down at the final table, but he had kept his eye on the play and was confident he could grind the guy down.

"Yo, what's your name playa?" his opponent asked.

"Steve, and you?" *Should I be giving out a fake name? No ... that would be an odd thing for an innocent person to do.*

"Shane. Listen, I'm high as fuck. How do you feel about doing a deal so we can both bounce? I'll split the rest of the prize money with ya."

"Thanks for the offer Shane, but I don't usually do deals. I think I'm good enough heads-up to win."

"Your call bro, but I am running hot," his opponent had said. He had cornrows and a tattoo of Tupac on his left bicep. He had double Steve's amount of chips, roughly 1 million to Steve's 500K.

After the player in third, a brown-haired lady wearing so

much jewellery she sounded like a wind chime, had her As Ad cracked by Shane's Jh 8d, Steve moved around the table to sit closer to his opponent. That way the dealer could get the cards out to each player faster and the hands would speed up. "All right if I sit here?" he said. He immediately regretted it when he smelt the stench of stale weed permeating from Shane.

"OK guys," said the dealer, "we're heads up, blinds are ten and twenty thousand, and there are no more antes. Good luck."

The dealer, who Steve couldn't help but compare to a stick insect, shuffled, then dealt. Steve looked down at 9d 9h and raised to 41K. He looked over at Shane who had Ad Js and decided to call.

"You feeling confident?" Shane said, "I've got my favourite hand."

The flop was Kc 9s 3s, and the action was on Shane. He checked it over to Steve. "I thought it was your favourite hand," said Steve, and smiled. "I was expecting you to bet." Steve bet 45K.

"You know what, this is my favourite hand. I'm all in." Shane replied.

He didn't have enough time to get his chips in before Steve had shouted "Call!" turned his cards over and thrown all his chips into the pot.

"Damn, I thought you had nothing!" Shane exclaimed. "It's still my favourite hand, though. I still believe." The dealer dealt the turn – Qh – and Steve's stomach lurched. He had a distinct feeling that his luck had just run out. Sure enough, 10d on the river gave Shane the straight, beating Steve's three of a kind, and he summarised the hand with a wide-eyed "Wow."

He stood up and stuck out a hand to Steve, who shook it and said, "Well played," without really meaning it. *How have I lost to this chump?* He couldn't explain the overwhelming feeling of injustice he felt. He opened the internet browser on his phone and did a quick search for a poker equity calculator; a tool to work out your percentage chance of winning. He filled the cards in, but it only served to fuel the intense feeling of frustration he had. *I was a ninety-eight per cent favourite to win when the chips went into the middle!*

They went to the registration desk and got their prize tickets to take to the cashier, standing next to each other at the desk in awkward silence. But Steve had still won a thousand pounds, and although the ending stung, he couldn't be too disappointed with the result. *I guess I can't do anything about luck with my glasses,* he thought, eyeing Shane. *Maybe I should have taken the deal.*

* * *

Steve walked over to Grant's table and stood behind the rail, the red lights indicating that filming was going on still shining brightly. There were three-of them left and they were standing around a laptop, in the process of discussing a deal themselves. "I don't know, mate," Grant was saying. "It seems like a lot to give up." He was facing the ponytailed guy, who had grown the mountain of chips in front of him.

"Well, it's fine by me. I say we shake hands." the third guy, a slender blonde with a thick Spanish accent, chimed in.

Then Grant spotted Steve. "Sorry guys, do you mind if I run it past my friend first?" They nodded agreement, and Grant motioned Steve away from the table.

"So, Ponytail wants to take £12K," he muttered, "but that's what first place gets, so he's basically saying I'm having first and you two can go fuck yourselves. He's been running hot, but everyone's stack is shallow. He can't outplay us because we're all going to be dictated to by the cards."

"What do second and third get?" Steve asked.

"Second gets £6K, third gets £4K."

"And the other guy is keen to deal?"

"Yes, he's just happy to get £5K and go."

Steve thought. "Do you think he'd give any more up?"

"Maybe," Grant said, scratching his stubbly beard. "I'd be happy with £6K."

"So, you could ask for £750 from Ponytail and £250 from the other guy, I guess but it depends how important the money is to you. Can you stomach going out in third and winning £4K, or is £5K going to have a significant impact on your life?"

Grant shifted from foot to foot. "It would make a huge difference," he said, rather reluctantly.

"So, do what you need to do, mate," said Steve. Grant walked back to the table. "I'm sure we can come to a deal here, chaps. I think I'm worth six thou in this situation, and I wonder if you'd be up for splitting the money between you." He faced Ponytail. "So, you give up £750 from what is first place." Then he faced the other man. "And you give up £250." He smiled. "I think that would mean we can all leave here happy."

Ponytail started talking first. "I'm not giving up £750, but I'll give you five hundred if he's willing to give up five hundred as well."

Grant looked at the other guy, who sighed. "Two-fifty I'll agree to, but I'm not giving up five hundred."

"Look, I'll take £5750, if you want to deal on that?" Everyone agreed and Grant smiled to himself. That was the fastest £750 he'd ever earned.

* * *

Steve and Grant walked over to the cashier together, both smiling. Steve couldn't help feeling he'd left some money on the table, though. He considered playing a cash table, but he was afraid of risking a lot of money when, as had happened before, things could go wrong. *Maybe I'll play cash when I've paid my debt off and won enough to keep me clear.* For now, a low-risk high-reward strategy was needed, which the tournaments provided. He looked at his watch. 11:30 pm, but he didn't feel like sleeping. *I suppose that's what happens when you're in a casino.*

"Fancy going for that beer?" Grant asked.

"Why not?" Steve replied.

* * *

They went to the casino bar, the only one likely to still be open this late on a Sunday, and got two beers.

"Sorry I missed you before the start of the tournament, mate," said Steve. "I had a few errands to run and I totally lost track of time."

"Don't worry about it," Grant said, staring into his beer.

Steve looked more closely at him. "You alright, mate? You don't seem your usual chipper self."

"Oh, I'm fine…" said Grant. Then he sighed and pulled at his beer. "Actually no, I'm not fine. Not at all." He looked Steve in the eye. "We found out the other day that my wife has motor neurone disease. The doctors reckon she could have two years left to live." Grant's voice broke on the last words. "I'm beside myself, but I daren't show it in front of her or the kids. I need

95

her to know that we'll be OK once she's … once she's gone. I'm trying to stay strong, but God, it's hard."

"Fucking hell, mate, that's horrendous." Steve got up from his chair and gave Grant a hug. Grant hugged him back a little less firmly. "If you ever need to chat, you know I'm only a phone call away."

"Thanks mate, I appreciate that." Grant started to sniff. *Oh no,* thought Steve. *How can I lighten the mood?*

"By the way, did I tell you I lost a heads-up match to a guy who was high as a kite?"

Grant laughed at him through the tears. "How'd you manage to mess that up?"

"The fellah ran like a God! Either that or the fumes coming from him got me high as well!"

Grant looked at him, his eyes kind. "It's nice to have a pal to talk about poker with in real life. I'm used to it just being little lines of text on the screen."

"Yeah well, I'm not the best player in the world so don't ask me anything too complicated!"

"Ha, says the guy who's two for two on getting heads up! You're playing at the wrong stakes, mate…"

They drank the last of their beers, and Steve could see Grant's head starting to nod with fatigue. "Come on mate, time to call it a night." He called Grant a cab and they waited outside for it to arrive, the rain falling lightly on the pavement.

Chapter 9

As Steve was packing his bag to go home on the Monday, he reflected on the weekend. He'd walked out with an extra £575, the 10% that Grant insisted on giving him, on top of the £1000 he'd won in the second tournament. He could knock almost 10% off the amount he owed. *Not a bad result for one weekend*, he thought.

But the idea of trying to use the glasses another ten or eleven times made him uneasy. He'd taken too many risks already. Winding the wiry guy up and getting punched, resulting in the glasses being knocked off his face; not to mention plotting and executing the theft of property from a casino.

Steve smiled as he repeated to himself: *I stole from a casino safe and got away with it.* But he couldn't do all that another ten times. He'd been lucky, but that luck would run out, especially if he pushed it. *I need to get into one tournament big enough to make it all back in one go.* He mused, packing the notes from his heist between the clothes in his bag. He couldn't leave them in the hotel bin. He'd get rid of them later.

He knew about satellite tournaments, where the ultimate prize was entry into a bigger tournament, but he'd never played one and didn't know much about the strategy, though he assumed it would be different from a normal tournament. As the top prizes were the same value, from first to however many entries were up for grabs, people might play more conservatively; they didn't need to win, just finish in the prizes. He could probably bluff people off hands more often when they had a weak but still better holding than he did, but would need to be more careful when he wanted them to call. *I need to work out how others will play so I can adjust my strategy.*

Steve counted the money out to make sure it was still all there, then tucked it into a pocket on the inside of his suitcase. He looked at the packs of cards and decided he could bin those. The hotel staff would probably think it a bit weird, but that would be all. He packed his laptop between a pair of shorts and a T-shirt to protect it from any bumps and checked out of the hotel. He had an evening shift at the supermarket but hopefully he could get back in time to see Tanya. He was sure she'd be happy he could pay some of the debt off early.

* * *

Steve returned home to find Tanya playing with the kids in the garden. She had the hose out and they were running through the stream. Steve grinned before stripping down to his boxers and picking up his daughters one by one to get a super-soaking. All his troubles melted away as they shrieked and giggled, and for the first time in a long time, they were all happy.

"Look at your shoulders, they're bright red," said Tanya, pointing. "Go and put some sun cream on, doofus, you're burning!"

Steve retreated into the kitchen to look for some and Tanya joined him, leaving the girls outside to spray each other with water. "So, how was the lads' weekend away?" she said, nudging him. "I hope you managed to steer clear of the gentlemen's clubs!" Not that Tanya would have minded if they had gone to a strip club; she knew he'd never cheat on her.

"It was pretty good," Steve replied. "We drank a lot of beer; it felt like I was at university again! We were in the pub most of Saturday, then went to a club that played heavy metal. Oh, and on Sunday we had a few beers and then went to the casino and played poker. And you'll never guess who won the tournament?"

"No way! You won it?" Tanya said, genuinely excited. "How much did you win?" Steve stopped looking for the sun cream and turned to face Tanya.

"Just under £1600. We can pay off some of the debt with it."

"Of course we can. Oh, well done, baby!" Tanya flung her arms around him and hugged him tightly. "Just promise if you go on another lads weekend that you won't lose too much. I don't want to take out another loan to pay off gambling losses."

"Don't worry, I won't," said Steve. "I only ever play poker, because it's the only game in the casino where you're not playing against the house. I've absolutely no interest in roulette or the slots." He paused, thinking. "They were actually using my tables in there, you know; they were really nice to play on." He couldn't keep the sadness out of his voice. *I wish I were still working on that project. I'd have loved to have been involved in optimising them and creating new designs...*

"Ahh, I'm sorry baby." Tanya squeezed him even tighter. "That must have been tough."

"It's alright. One of the lads, Grant, told me his wife's just been diagnosed with motor neurone disease, and that's put my troubles into perspective. I couldn't imagine losing you or one of the kids."

"Oh no, that's terrible news. That poor man." Steve looked Tanya in the eyes, his heart bursting. *I'll get rid of this debt, and then the glasses are gone,* he thought.

* * *

The following day, Steve got into the Astra and pulled out of his drive. He noticed a black SUV with tinted windows parked across the road as he drove off to work. *Huh, the Bensons must have got a new car.* Tanya was going to visit her father with the kids and was due to set off shortly after he'd left. Steve felt guilty that he hadn't been to see George for a while and silently promised himself he'd try to go and see him. *I'm not sure how much more time I can spend on the tills. I wonder if they'll let me swap to shelf-stacking instead. Maybe I could have a go at the online picking actually, it looks like it might be quite good fun running around the store with a trolley picking people's shopping for them, a bit like Supermarket Sweep. Oooh I like this song!* Steve thought, as Iron Maiden came on the car radio.

* * *

At the end of Steve's shift, he spotted the same black SUV he'd seen that morning parked a few spaces away from him in the car park. He drove deliberately slowly out of the car park, watching the SUV. It didn't move from its parking space and Steve's momentary unease disappeared. He wound the windows down and turned Metallica up loud, singing along.

As he pulled up onto the drive, Steve noticed the front door was ajar. Tanya wasn't supposed to be back until later, the kids

100

had swimming lessons and they usually went out for dinner after. "Hello!" he shouted as he got out of the car, but there was no reply.

Steve pushed the door open slowly. "Oh fuck!" he shouted as he peered into the hallway. Their belongings were strewn everywhere, and the cupboard doors were open. Steve covered his mouth with his hands as he looked at the devastation. *The glasses!* He raced up the stairs, dodging the children's toys, and ran into his and Tanya's room. His suitcase, which he hadn't unpacked, was open, and had clearly been rifled through. *They wouldn't have thought to try the glasses on, surely.* He pulled the clothes out frantically and breathed a huge sigh of relief when he found the glasses in their case at the bottom. *The money! Steve* unzipped the pocket where he'd stashed it and stuck his hand in, expecting to find nothing.

What the fuck? Steve pulled out a wad of notes and counted it. When he had finished, stacks of notes were piled on the floor in front of him. It was all there; the weekend's winnings, as well as the cash he'd won at the first tournament. *What kind of robber turns a place over and misses all that cash?* He went downstairs, and the television was still on the stand. *What about my laptop?* he thought surprised by his own lack of concern. *If they have taken it, they'll have a hard time cracking my password, and they definitely won't know what the glasses software is.* He ran back to his suitcase and pulled everything out, but his laptop was gone. *Maybe that was all they were looking for.*

Steve smiled. He'd stored the program he'd written for the glasses in an online repository, behind a wall of security. *I won't even have to rewrite it.* He sighed with relief, then clenched his fists. *OK, time to call it in.* Steve called the police, and then called Tanya to let her know the bad news.

* * *

The police turned up twenty minutes later; a man and a woman wearing bright yellow high-vis police vests and belts with various weapons and tools.

"Hello, are you Mr Ash?" the female officer called out. "We've had a report of a burglary."

No, thought Steve, *I'm the remarkably irritated burglar casually trying to make my way through the carnage I've just created.* He sighed. "Yes, that's me. They've turned every room over, as far as I can see."

"All right sir, would you mind coming over here and answering a few questions?" the male officer asked. He had a well-kept black beard and a strong jaw; he would have been perfect for a razor blade commercial. "What time did you leave the house this morning, and when did you get back?"

"Around half seven, but my wife was here later. I'm not sure when she left exactly." Steve replied. He noticed the female officer looking through the windows of the house before disappearing down the side of the building.

"All right. What time did you get home?"

"Four pm."

"And which rooms have you entered since returning?"

Steve thought. "The hallway, the living room and my bedroom."

"Ok, and have you noticed anything is missing?"

"Actually, just my laptop. They turned the place over, but they missed the cash in my suitcase and left the TVs."

"That's interesting," said the policeman, scribbling furiously in his notepad. "It's good that you haven't been in all of the rooms. That will give forensics a chance to get some decent results." He looked up. "How much cash did you have in the suitcase?"

For a moment Steve considered lying. Then he shrugged. "£2200, just about."

The policeman's eyes narrowed. "Just for my benefit," he said slowly, "why do you have £2200 in cash in a suitcase?"

"I can see how that might sound a bit suspicious," Steve gabbled. "I just got back from a weekend away playing poker. I won the tournament, you see."

"Well done," remarked the policeman. "Did you notice anything suspicious when you left the house this morning?"

Steve looked up the road. The black SUV he had seen this morning was gone. "It might be nothing, but I saw a black SUV parked here this morning. Then I saw the same car parked at the supermarket I work at when I left this afternoon. It didn't follow me here or anything, but I've never seen one around here before, and the day I'm burgled I see it at the start and end of the day."

"Mmmm," said the policeman, writing it down. "Did you get a reg number? Make and model?"

"No, sorry," said Steve, kicking himself for not paying more attention.

"OK, that's all I can do till forensics get here," the policeman replied, in a monotone. "If you do see the same car again take a note of the number plate and we'll send someone round to ask a few questions."

The female officer reappeared. "They've turned the place over pretty well. That's good as far as forensics are concerned, there's more chance of them finding something."

Just as the two officers got into their car to leave, Tanya drove up the road. She had a mint-green Fiat 500 which was just about big enough for the kids' car seats. It was a tight squeeze, but Tanya loved it, and had named it Bauer after Jack Bauer from *24*. She parked quickly, and Steve could see her saying something to the kids. Then she jumped out and ran to Steve. "Did they take any of Mum's jewellery?" she cried.

"I don't know, I didn't see." Steve replied. He looked at Bauer. "I don't think we should let the kids see this mess; it might make them scared to come in."

Tanya nodded. "To be honest, it's freaking me out. I'll find us a hotel room for tonight." She glanced at the car, then back at Steve. "Will you be OK to stay here and sort it all out?"

"Yes, course I will. I'm not sure how long the police are going to be."

"OK. Love you." She hugged Steve tight and Steve felt his heart bursting with love. She really meant it. It was the first time he'd felt secure of that since James had screwed him over. *We're going to be* OK, he thought, and it was like a weight lifting. He popped his head in through the car window as Tanya got into the driver's side.

"Girls, Mummy is taking you out on a little adventure tonight. But you need to be as good as gold for her, because we're both feeling a little bit sad at the moment. Is that ok?" Steve said, trying to speak in a softer tone than usual.

"Why are you sad?" Fiona asked, with big, scared eyes. *Not the right choice of words, Steve.*

"You know when someone snatches a toy from you, and it makes you upset? Well, some nasty person has done that to Mummy and Daddy."

"Oh. Are the police going to catch the bad person?" Fiona asked.

"Yes, they are, and they'll lock him in prison." Steve said

firmly. Then he opened the passenger doors and gave both the girls a hug and a kiss. He watched them drive off, then turned his attention back to the house. It took an hour for the forensic scientist to arrive, dressed in a mustard-yellow jumpsuit. As soon as he got out of the car he put the jumpsuit hood up and pulled the drawstring tight, then put on a mask and went into the house, with barely a word to Steve other than to find out which rooms hadn't been compromised. *He looks a bit like Walter White, I hope he doesn't try and cook meth while he's in there.*

* * *

Steve hung around outside his own house for what felt like an eternity, longing to get changed out of his work uniform and start cleaning up. He ordered a pizza to be delivered to the house and intercepted the driver as he stopped on the pavement, eyes drawn to the sight of the forensics van. Steve paid, took the pizza, and got into his car. He had just taken a slice of pizza when a notification popped up on his phone, 'Dr Ibben has just gone live!'. Steve could still connect to the house Wi-Fi, so he opened the notification to see Grant sitting at a desk. "What's up poker patients, the Doctor is in session!" Grant cried. *He's certainly an entertainer.*

The view switched from the webcam to a view of the virtual table where Grant was playing online poker. His opponent's avatars were spread around the oval green table, above a number showing their chip stack. Steve could see what Grant's cards were, and as the hands played out Grant explained what he was thinking. His webcam had moved to the top right of the screen, and whilst it was small on Steve's phone, he could see him jumping around when a hand got exciting. Steve watched Grant play and couldn't help but feel slightly envious of how good he was. He was eerily skilled at working out what hands people had, and whilst he didn't always get the chance to see his opponents' cards, he was so often right that it didn't matter. It was almost like he had Steve's glasses, but online.

As the sun was setting, the forensic scientist came outside. He removed his mask and approached the car. "I've taken lots of photos, but I didn't find anything DNA-wise except a few hairs that look like they belong to a dog. Do you have a dog?" Steve shook his head. "Didn't think so, as there weren't any dog bowls or food in the house. Whoever did the job here was clearly a professional, Weird that he left the TV's and all that money though. If we find anything then you'll hear back from the police at some point if it leads anywhere."

"Ok, cheers mate," Steve replied, not quite knowing what to say, and the forensics guy walked to his van without saying anything further. Steve walked back in through the front door and looked at the belongings scattered everywhere. *Right, suppose I should do one room at a time.* He put Grant's stream on the TV in the living room and started to tidy up. Steve had managed to make most of the ground floor look normal when he went back into the living room to see Grant's grinning face. "All right patients, we are at the final table and there's a sweet ten grand at the top that we need to take with us. Let's send the rest of these guys to the rail."

He was the chip leader of the tournament and he knew how to play it, leaving the short stacks to double up when they went all in, and constantly going all in against the middle stacks to put them under pressure. That was an effective strategy; the middle stacks didn't want to bust before one of the short stacks, who were likely to bust soon, and receive a lower prize. Even if they did have a hand and called Grant, he knew he wouldn't bust, which took the pressure off him. Inevitably the short stacks did bust, which gave him fewer people he could use the tactic against. Now he either needed to outplay his opponents or make some hands. *Come on Grant,* willed Steve. *You can do it, mate.*

Grant had a live heart monitor on at the bottom of the screen, which had stayed pretty steady at 65 beats per minute, but when he was dealt the Ks Kc in the big blind, with three players left, it began to spike, as high as 150 bpm. The button folded and the small blind, who had around 20 big blinds, decided to play it simple and go all in.

Grant snap-called and was up against Ah 9d. The flop appeared on the screen: 6d 8c 9s. "HOLD IT!" Grant shouted. The 6s appeared. "HOLD!" he shouted again. 3h appeared on the river and Grant jumped out of his seat cheering. Steve found himself on his feet cheering too, arms in the air. "Get in there!" he shouted. His final opponent offered up a deal which Grant turned down. It felt inevitable that he was going to win. Grant's opponent had thirty big blinds and he had one hundred and ten.

Two hands passed without incident before Grant was dealt 10d 10h. "OK, so we've got pocket tens here in the big blind. If we see a raise, we're definitely going to three-bet." The other player did raise, and Grant followed through. His opponent decided to call. "OK, we're going to a flop. Boom! We've flopped top set with our pocket tens on the ten of spades, seven of hearts, eight of spades board. We're going to bet here and continue our aggression post-flop." He paused, thinking, then continued, almost to himself. "We're always getting called by hands like jacks and queens that might have called pre-flop, and some hands with a seven, eight or ten in them. How sweet would it be if they had two pairs with seven-eight?"

Grant carried on talking as he waited for his opponent to act, the heart rate on his monitor maintaining a steady 150. Suddenly the opponent went all in and Grant snap called. His opponent had 8s 8h for a set, but he was behind and needed to hit the final 8 in the deck to win. "Holy shit, he's only got one out, LET'S HOLD IT!"

Steve saw a woman and two girls walk in behind him. *That must be Rebecca and his daughters.* "How's it going?" she asked, but Grant was focused on the cards.

The turn appeared: Ad. "Come on, we need to fade one card for ten bags... YEAHHHHHHH!" Grant shouted as the Qc appeared on the screen. He jumped out of his chair, clocking his wife and children behind him. "I JUST WON TEN GRAND!" They jumped up and down in celebration together, shouting and screaming.

Steve pogoed up and down in the middle of his living room. He grabbed hold of his phone and texted Grant. *Well done mate! £16K in one week, can't be bad!* Then he sat down on the sofa, gripped by a new sense of motivation. He took out his phone and started browsing for poker schedules at the various casinos he knew he could play at with his glasses. It took about five minutes before the answer jumped out at him. The JUKPT was running in two weeks at Jacques Casino Nottingham, with live satellites every day. It cost a thousand pounds to enter the main event, but the satellites were only a hundred, which was within Steve's budget. The prize pool guarantee was half a million, which meant that first place would probably be around £50,000. *This is the one,* thought Steve. *I can run the glasses one more time, and then I'm out.*

Chapter 10

Eddie Liddell sat in his office at Jacques Casino HQ, based in the office block above the Nottingham casino. He was short, but extremely broad, and worked out every day. His physique was the thing he was the proudest of, and years of boxing had made him good at taking and throwing a punch. He was Area Manager for the Midlands and covered the biggest casinos in the Jacques portfolio. Eddie practically lived in his office, which was spotless, nevertheless. In pride of place on the wall was a portrait of Alexander Jacques. Today, he was reviewing Saturday morning's CCTV tapes of the card room at Nottingham. He thought back to the events that had led him to looking at these particular tapes. Ron Jacobs, one of the card-room managers, had turned up to the head office uninvited, and ambushed Eddie whilst he was making his morning espresso.

"Hi Eddie, how's it going?" Ron asked.

"Yeah, all right… Ron Jacobs, right? What brings you here today?"

"Can I mention something to you … off the record?"

"Of course. Shall we go to my office?"

"Sure." They walked across the main office to Eddie's door. The floor was quiet; some monitors were occupied by staff, but the majority were clear. Monday mornings were always quiet for casinos. They walked in and Eddie closed the door. All the glass was frosted, to prevent people from seeing what Eddie was doing.

Eddie sat down in his plush leather office chair and motioned for Ron to sit on the other side of the desk. "What's troubling you, Ron?"

"I think someone cheated at poker over the weekend. It's more of a feeling than anything, I can't really prove it."

"OK ... what makes you think they cheated?"

"As I said, I can't explain it. The person who came second in our side event seemed a bit... shady. I'm sure he works for the new company that's building us the tables. He introduced himself as Steve, and when I looked him up on our computer, he's called Steve Ash. He was the spitting image of the guy who came to replace the playing cards, you know, James Baldwin. Just seems a bit weird that the company name is Baldwin and Ash, y'know."

Eddie held up his hands. "Whoa, whoa, let's just wind back a second. What guy who came to replace the cards? Nobody was supposed to be replacing anything this weekend."

The colour drained from Ron's face. "A guy came into the casino. He had a briefcase ... he had Alexander Jacques's phone number..."

"Ron, what did you give him?"

"He just wanted the marked cards, no cash or anything." Ron swallowed. "So, I got them out of the safe, and — Oh my God, I'm so sorry..."

Eddie's mind was racing. "Didn't you ask him for ID?" *He'd better answer with a yes, otherwise he's out.*

"He told me he'd left it at a coffee shop on his way from

London."

"RON!" Eddie stood up, tipping his office chair over behind him. "We don't let people gamble their own money without an ID. We definitely don't let them into our safes without ID." He paced up and down behind the desk, trying to contain his anger. "Your job's gone; you know that?"

Ron stared at him. "But I've done the right thing coming forward!"

"Don't fucking push it, pal. You'd best fuck off right now before I do something I regret," Eddie seethed. Ron had left without a word, and it had taken Eddie about an hour to calm down.

Face-recognition software was in place across all Jacques casinos, and it had taken five minutes to work out that the guy who had been in that morning was the same person who'd played the tournament that afternoon. Eddie wrote the name *Steve Ash* on his whiteboard, with a CCTV shot of him stuck above it.

Eddie had no desire to report Steve to the police, quite the opposite, in fact. What many people didn't know about the Jacques family was that the casinos were a front for what they considered their real business. Their casino empire was the biggest money-laundering operation in the UK, and Eddie was responsible for making sure it operated efficiently. The last thing he wanted was the police coming in and asking questions. However, part of his job was to stop people cheating the casino's. Honest winning was fine, welcome even; once they'd experienced that high, Eddie wanted them to return and give it all back chasing the euphoria. It was the snakes that came in and tried to cheat the games that really made his blood boil. The most blatant were the people counting cards at blackjack; Eddie had lost count of the people he'd caught doing that, thinking they were smart enough to get away with it. He usually just threw them out of the casino; it was only when he didn't know *how* they were cheating that they'd be taken for interrogation. Poker didn't usually cause him any problems, but this was the second issue flagged up this month. Eddie was going to get to the bottom of it, and fast.

* * *

The following night, Eddie's phone rang. It was an unsaved number, which usually meant the Russian, the man he'd hired to search Steve Ash's house for some clue as to how he was pulling off the scam. "I'm here," a thick Russian accent said, and the line went dead. Eddie grabbed the £3,000 he'd promised from the safe behind Alexander's portrait, all in fifties bound together just like in a bank, and put it in his jacket pocket. Then he walked out to the casino car park, where a black SUV was waiting. The lights flashed on and off, and Eddie got into the passenger seat.

"I tore the place limb from limb, but I couldn't find anything obvious." The driver didn't look at Eddie when he spoke. He wore a black unbranded hoody, with the hood up, and black jogging bottoms. His thick Russian accent was the only remarkable thing about him. The car smelt slightly of dog; Eddie had an idea what the dog might be for, but had never been in a situation yet which had required the use of one. Things had never got to that level.

The Russian reached into the back seat and passed Eddie a cheap-looking black rucksack. Eddie opened it. Inside was a laptop and some sheets of paper that had clearly been torn from a notepad.

Eddie held a page up to the floodlight. On it were a list of shops: a suit shop, a wig shop and a games store. "That is where the dog is buried." The Russian said without looking at Eddie. Eddie grunted, then put the page back into the bag, zipped it up, and handed over the cash. He got out of the car, hefted the rucksack, and went back to his office. There, he plugged the laptop in and switched it on. Whilst it started, he walked to the office kitchen and began to make coffee. Eddie was a coffee snob, and had got an expensive filter coffee machine for the office. He poured water in, popped in a filter, and spooned in Kopi Luwak coffee. *Gross really, the coffee cherries are eaten and defecated by civets. Yet it's the most expensive coffee in the world, £250 for a bag, so there must be something about it.*

Eddie switched the machine on, and it groaned into life, steaming hot water starting to drip from the filter into the jug below. *I wonder what Steve Ash's new password should be. Maybe 'EddieLiddellisthebest' or 'IthoughtIcouldstealfromJacques. Nah, they're too boring. Hmm... What about 'HittheRoadJacques!'*

Whilst the coffee brewed, Eddie walked back to his office, humming Ray Charles to himself. He plugged a USB stick into the laptop and set it to restart, then switched it into boot mode and loaded a system based on the USB stick. *This is so easy; I don't know why films make out this takes a lot of skill. Actually, I can't even be bothered making this password complicated.* He switched into administrator mode and changed the password on the account 'Steve Ash' to IMACHEATER. Eddie restarted the computer and let it load normally, before retyping the password. Hey presto, he was into Steve's laptop.

Steve's wallpaper was a photo of a brown-haired woman in her late thirties with two young brown-haired girls, standing outside a manor house with ice creams dripping down their hands. *There's a family, good to know,* he thought, and saved the picture to his USB drive to print later. He walked back to the kitchen, poured his coffee, and took a sip before running to the sink to spit it out. *It actually tastes like shit. What a waste of money!* Eddie poured the rest of the jug down the sink before changing the filter and starting the process again, this time with his Italian roast coffee beans.

* * *

Eddie wasn't often surprised, but it did shock him to find specifications for the tables, cameras and original cards on Steve's laptop. *This must be the Ash of 'Baldwin and Ash',* he thought. He snapped Steve's CCTV picture of with his phone and sent it to Alexander Jacques on WhatsApp, with the caption 'Recognise him?'. *I love their end-to-end encryption.*

Alexander phoned five minutes later. "He's the guy James dumped from the tables business. Steve something. Why's he on your radar?"

"He blagged his way into the card room pretending to be James, and fooled the card-room manager at Nottingham into giving him packs of the new cards." Eddie paused. "And it gets worse. He's played three tournaments in the last two months. Didn't cash in the one just before he got the new cards. But guess what, he comes first and second in the two either side. He's cheating, must be."

"Fucking hell, I didn't think he had it in him. Work out how he is doing it, and call me back." Alexander hung up. Eddie found a picture of James and added it to the web of contacts on his whiteboard with some notes on Baldwin and Ash Gaming

Tables Ltd. The picture was starting to build. He did some digging around on the internet and found a programme called Lens Uploader which sounded like something Steve might have used to upload the card patterns. *But to where?* Eddie mulled the question over, and wrote down a few theories. *Could he be using a phone? How?*

Eddie scratched his head, frowning, then relaxed. He didn't need to chase Steve. All he had to do was let Steve come into the casino, watch what he was doing, and let him give himself away. He put an alert on Steve's account: *Notify me when this customer comes in.* Then he closed the laptop and turned to the casino's CCTV monitors. He watched the blackjack tables, noticing a Chinese man who moved his lips whenever a picture card or low card was dealt. Eddie sighed before getting up from his desk and heading downstairs to throw him out.

Chapter 11

"Did you enjoy the pyjama party daddy?" Fiona asked. Steve was wearing pyjamas for what had felt like the first time in years. All three of the girls had insisted he join them, and he'd quite enjoyed busting out the dad dancing.

"Absolutely, we should do it again soon. Now though, it's time for sleep. Goodnight, darling." Steve said to Fiona.

"Are you and Mummy friends again now?" Fiona asked. *Whoa, where did that come from?*

"We've always been friends, darling, what made you think we weren't?"

"Sometimes I hear you arguing. It sounds like you're both angry and it makes me sad." She cuddled her bunny, Teddy, tighter as she looked at her dad with eyes that could melt the coldest of hearts.

"Sometimes your mum and I disagree about things, and occasionally we get cross with each other, but we always make friends in the end. I'm really sorry it's made you sad though. I promise it won't happen again."

"Okay, I love you Daddy."

"I love you too," he said, giving her one last hug and kiss before leaving the room and switching the light off. *I need to get rid of this debt.* Steve walked down the stairs and into the living room where Tanya was sitting on the sofa in her elephant pyjamas, nursing a glass of red wine. She had her legs curled up underneath her, and she smiled at Steve as he poured a glass for himself, before topping Tanya's up and sitting down next to her.

"Fiona was worried we weren't friends. She said she'd heard us arguing."

Tanya looked at Steve, concerned. "What did you tell her?"

"I just said sometimes we disagreed, but we always made friends in the end. I promised her she wouldn't hear us shouting at each other again."

"OK, that's a deal." She took Steve's hand and they watched TV for a while before Steve broke the silence.

"I've been invited away with some of the lads from work to Nottingham next weekend," he said. "There's a poker festival going on over three days called the True Grinder Series... They'll probably do some other things like paintball and biking around Sherwood Forest too. Would you mind if I tagged along?"

Tanya frowned. "How much is the tournament?"

"Well, some of us are going to try and satellite into one that's a grand."

"It's going to cost you a grand?"

"No, it'll cost a hundred pounds. The prize for the hundred-pound tournament is entry into a thousand-pound tournament."

"I don't mind, but don't blow all your money, will you?" she said before taking a swig from her glass.

"I promise I'll be sensible." Steve could tell she wasn't very happy about it, and he decided not to say any more about it for now. "I love you, y'know."

"I love you too."

* * *

The week between getting permission from Tanya and actually getting ready to go seemed to take forever. But Thursday had finally arrived, and Steve loaded the car up for his last poker trip with the glasses. His plan was to go up and win the satellite on Thursday, and then play the tournament across Friday, Saturday, and Sunday. He'd carry on playing after this tournament, but this would be the last time he'd use the glasses. *I'm not going to be one of those people who gets too greedy and loses it all.* Grant had won a satellite online and was going to meet Steve on the first day of the main event. A three-dayer would be a new experience for Steve; he'd never played a tournament longer than two days.

Steve felt guilty when he thought of the lies he'd told — of course there was no paintball or Sherwood Forest trip planned — and he promised himself that would be the last time he'd do it. He knew Tanya would never condone the use of the glasses, but he owed it to her and the kids to get them out of the hole he'd got them all into.

* * *

Steve sat in the Astra, gripped the steering wheel, and closed his eyes. The last few months had been exhausting, and he was ready for it to be over. He'd never thought it would be the case, but he seriously missed his old job as an analyst. At least then he'd earned a decent wage, worked normal hours, and had normal stress levels.

Steve turned the ignition key and the Vauxhall came to life, growling moodily in the September sunshine. The car pulled off the drive, and Steve drove absentmindedly to the apartment he'd booked. When he arrived, he was disappointed. The pictures on the website were clearly of a different flat, and the description had failed to mention that paint was peeling from the walls, the air stank of cigarettes, and the flat was directly opposite a strip club. It had been cheap, though, which had been his main criteria.

Steve went into the bedroom, put down his suitcase, and looked out of the window. The strip club was painted entirely black. Neon lights above the door, currently switched off, spelt out 'Beavers'. *Charming*, Steve thought. He went to the Lyle's convenience store he'd seen on the corner and stocked up. His fridge filled with pizza, beer, and some milk to go with his cereal for the mornings, he walked to the casino.

* * *

Steve walked through the main atrium of the casino, past the millions of brightly lit slot machines with their irritatingly catchy tunes. The card room was about a quarter full of people playing cash, the clicking and clacking of chips louder than their conversation. Steve decided to go and watch, not because he was interested in the hands that they were playing, but because he'd learnt from his previous mistake. The cards he had registered in the glasses were picking up perfectly. He walked around all the tables, watching a few hands on each and making sure that the cards in the shuffle masters were ones he could see. Of the eight decks he watched, there was only one set he couldn't see, but that was good enough for him. He strolled to the desk. "I'd like to register for the satellite, please."

"Absolutely," said the clerk behind the desk. "Can I have your membership card, please?"

Steve handed his card over and the man swiped it down the side of the kiosk. Then he frowned, waiting for confirmation.

"Everything OK, mate?" Steve asked, as casually as he could. The man didn't respond; he was still watching his screen. Then he looked at Steve and smiled broadly.

"All OK." He handed Steve a receipt. "Sorry for the wait, mate. The computer was having a bit of a senior moment."

Steve wandered over to the bar to get himself a drink. He looked around, his back to the bar. The room was brightly lit, with no window in sight. It could easily be the middle of the night outside, and you'd never know. "I'll have a pint of Jackpot please." Steve asked when the bartender came over to him. The beer was hoppy, refreshing and invigorating. He took a big draught of it before walking over to the table he was playing at and relaxing into a plush leather chair.

To Steve's surprise, there were only six people registered for the tournament, all of them sat at his table. It didn't seem like many compared to usual, especially as two seats had been guaranteed for the prize pool. *The prize pool is two thousand and they've only collected six hundred. Maybe they've overpromised.* The cards lay face-up in the middle of the table, for the players to check none were missing. The dealer swiped them up, shuffled, then dealt like a man possessed.

Steve looked at his cards: 9s 2s. *Fuck it, let's get off to a good start.* He raised from middle position to 300 and was three-bet by the player on the button, who held As 5s, and raised to

900. Steve called the raise, and they saw a flop of 6s 7h 8s. *It's pretty well coordinated, but this board definitely suits me more than someone who's three-bet. I can check-call on the flop and turn, then check-raise on the river if there's no spade and no ace.*

Steve executed the first part of his plan, calling the 1200 bet. He looked at his chips, already down to just under 8000. *Bloody hell, this stack is short. I can see how they're making the guarantee: re-entries.* The turn was Jc, a safe card for Steve's plan. His opponent didn't bet again, though, seemingly keen to keep the pot small himself.

The river was Qd, and Steve reassessed his plan. His opponent probably wouldn't bet; he'd missed all his draws and was probably only getting called by hands that beat him. Steve had a vague feeling he'd played this guy before, but couldn't place exactly where. His gut instinct was to bet big, so he bet 4000 chips, pushing in half of his stack. *I haven't thought about this. I should have just gone all in. What's the point in betting half my stack? Please, please fold! He tried not to panic as he watched his opponent.*

His opponent looked at his cards, sighed and said, "I don't know how I missed." throwing his cards face-up for everyone to see. *I played this guy in Luton, he's the unluckiest player in the world!* Steve scooped in the pot, a slight chuckle sneaking out.

* * *

It didn't take long before his first opponent had busted, and he re-entered. Then something unexpected happened. Dylan Broadmoor, the brash American he'd seen playing on TV, walked past the table and registered for the satellite. He sat down, two seats to Steve's right, then removed his enormous headphones and took his hoody off to reveal a large hockey jersey. The Vegas Golden Knights logo was printed across the middle; a spartan helmet, half-black, half-gold. *He's not as intimidating in real life as he looks on TV. He's not as big either.*

"All right, Dylan?" Steve piped up. "What on earth are you doing here?"

"Hi, buddy," Dylan replied, taking being recognised in his stride. "I've just signed a new sponsorship deal with Jacques, and that means I've got to play the main event of the True Grinder. They paid for one entry, but I'm trying to get as many tickets as I can." His American accent marked him out distinctly from the rest of the players there.

"Well, good luck." Steve said.

"Thank you." Dylan replied. *Oh, I want to outplay this guy*, thought Steve. *I'd love to be on the end of one of his rants!*

Dylan Broadmoor was quiet and didn't play many hands across the first few orbits. He seemed to be trying to get a feel for how the others were playing. Steve had done the opposite, playing almost every hand looking for opportunities to bluff people out. He'd done it so successfully that he hadn't had to showdown anything except the one time he'd had a hand, making a straight with Kc Qd. He'd built his stack up to a comfortable 30K, and with the blinds at 400/200 he was easily the chip leader. Quite a few more players had joined, and the casino had opened another table. A few of the short-stacked players had been moved to the other table, which was good for Steve. It was harder to bluff people who were likely to become easily committed to the pot.

* * *

123

Steve really wanted to play a hand with Dylan and eventually he obliged, but it didn't go the way Steve wanted. He called a bet of 800 with 7s 8s against Dylan's Qs Qd. *Well, it's not every day you get to play with Dylan Broadmoor,* he thought. The flop was good for Steve, with Kc 6c 9d appearing in the middle of the felt. Steve decided he would call one time when Dylan bet. Dylan bet 1200 and Steve, following through on his plan.

The turn was Js. Steve decided he would either bet or raise, depending on Dylan's next move. If he had to, he was happy to go big and get the job done on the river. Dylan hesitated, then checked. Steve bet 2500 and after sighing, Dylan called.

The river was 10h, a terrible card for Steve. He'd made a straight, but Dylan had the higher end of the straight and there was no way he would fold now. Dylan announced he was all in, and this time it was Steve's turn to sigh. When he folded, Dylan jumped out of his chair. "Boom! Nobody here can outplay Broadmoor when he's got his A-game out!" *You got lucky on the river, you idiot,* Steve thought.

* * *

They played on through the next hour, but very few people seemed to get knocked out. Dylan continued shouting whenever he won a pot; every twenty minutes or so he was shouting 'Boom!' or 'That's how it goes, baby!' and it was really winding Steve up. *Who does this guy think he is, and why does he have to shout all the time? I'm going to bring him down a peg or two.* The tournament director announced the last hand before the break and Steve found himself in the big blind, with the blinds now 600/300 and an ante of 600. Dylan opened the action on the button with As 7s to 1500. The small blind folded and Steve looked at his cards: Qd 8d. *Alright, let's have it.*

Steve called and did a double take when he saw the flop; 3d 5d 7d, giving Dylan top pair and top kicker, and Steve a queen-high flush. Steve was first to act, and as the rest of the players left the table, he decided to play in an unorthodox fashion, leading out for 800 into the 3900 pot. He had seen people do this when they were on a draw, trying to lead with a small amount so that they could see the next card cheaply. He figured Dylan might think that was his strategy and raise with his top pair in case there were more diamonds on the turn or river, making it easier for Steve to have a flush.

"No way I'm letting you get away with that," said Dylan, grinning. "What do you think I am, some kind of chump?" he said. Steve shrugged. *That's exactly what I think you are.* "I raise to 3500!" Dylan said, piling chips up in a tower. He pushed them forward, trying to make the bet look intimidating, but in truth the big stack of chips was made up mostly of 100s. Steve pretended to mull the decision over in his head, making a point of checking his cards. He gently pulled his chips back and replaced his small bet of 800 with 3500. The dealer scooped both bets into the pot and dealt the turn: Kh. Steve checked and Dylan watched him. "What's your name, pal?"

Steve met his eyes. "Steve."

"Well listen here, Steve, I've been playing this game for a long time and I don't want you to do anything you might regret, so I'm gonna give you some advice. That king is a great card for me, so when I bet it, you should probably be folding. Your pair of fives is no good here." He counted out a bet of 5000, leaving just 7000 in his stack. He pushed the chips forward and looked at Steve, who met his gaze. They locked eyes for what seemed like an age before, very coolly, Dylan said, "This is where you fold."

Steve felt a sudden rush of anger. *Why do people think they can bully me into doing things? Fuck this guy.* He turned to the dealer; "I'm all in."

Dylan slumped back in his chair. "There's no way you've got a flush here. Who leads with a made hand when the board is monotone? You should just trap." He tossed the rest of his chips in before turning away from the table in disgust at the sight of Steve's cards. There were no cards left that could save him. The river was dealt as Dylan got up from the table, but it didn't matter what it was. Steve had just knocked Dylan Broadmoor out of a poker tournament.

But Dylan wasn't finished. "You're a terrible player. How can you call that pre-flop when I've been playing so tight? You're a jackass, a total jackass. Enjoy the chips, maybe you can use them to get your family's teeth sorted." He didn't wait for Steve to reply, instead marching over to the registration desk to re-enter the tournament. *There's nothing wrong with our teeth, thanks!* Steve smiled to himself. As he watched Dylan flounce off, Steve couldn't believe what had just happened. He couldn't help but feel gutted that it had happened just before the break, as the other players, wandering off to go to the toilet or for a cigarette, had missed it. So instead, he called Grant. "You'll never guess who I just knocked out of the satellite! Dylan Broadmoor is here!" Steve said, before Grant could even say hello.

"No way!" said Grant. "You're pulling my leg. Why the hell would *he* be in Nottingham?"

"Apparently Jacques are sponsoring him. He called me a *jackass!*" Steve laughed as he tried to replicate Dylan's accent. "But what's a man to do when he flops a queen high flush?"

"Well, hopefully I'll get his table in the main event, so I can get some abuse when I beat him as well!" Grant's voice lowered. "Listen mate, we're in the waiting room at the hospital so I have to go. Nothing to worry about, just a routine check-up for Rebecca. I'll catch you tomorrow."

"No problem, mate, see you then." Steve said before the call ended. He hadn't realised beating Dylan was on his bucket list, but he really felt like he'd ticked something off. Despite all the abuse Dylan had given him, Steve couldn't help but admire the guy for being himself on screen. He clearly didn't care what people thought of him.

Steve walked around the card room, his glasses occasionally picking up cards. The break was soon over, though, and Steve sat back down in his seat, ready to play. He had 45K, and the average was just over 20K. There were 14 players left, and the two-seats guarantee had just been met, with a third-place prize of £120.

* * *

There were plenty of short stacks now, and it didn't take long before they were playing the final table. Dylan had managed to get a double-up, and everyone knew about it. As his opponent was walking away from the table, he yelled, "Played him like the fiddle that he is!" Steve wondered if Dylan had any friends. He could certainly see why he was being sponsored; he was irritating to play against, but entertaining to watch. He was good at poker too; despite whining about how bad everyone else was, he usually knew if he had the best hand or not.

Steve watched Dylan play a few hands and scoop pots in. Most he'd had the best hand for, but on one he bluffed all-in on the turn representing a flush. He was great at telling stories with his bets as well as his speech. He'd shown the bluff after his opponent had folded, shouting, "Feel the burn, baby!" You didn't need glasses that could see the cards to know his opponent had folded the winning hand.

Steve had managed to pick some chips up from the other players, specifically targeting those with a medium stack as his research had told him to do. He put them under pressure by making big bets when they didn't have anything decent, and giving up quickly when they made a better hand than he did. He took care not to go to showdown with his cards; he didn't want anyone to see the rubbish cards he was playing and aiming to maintain a reputation of consistently making hands and being aggressive with them. It had been much easier to push people around. Lots had been playing not to bust, trying to wait for a pair of aces, kings or queens. But eventually the blinds caught up with them, and they were forced to take a risk.

It wasn't long before they were down to four players: Steve, Dylan and two elderly grey-haired gentlemen. Steve felt it was most likely to be him and Dylan winning the tickets, unless the two older guys got a run of strong hands against Dylan. They had been too passive, and only seemed to get aggressive when they had the best hands it was possible to make. They certainly hadn't done any bluffing. It was just a case of grinding them down.

Steve was dealt Ah Js on the button and he raised to 5000 from his stack of 80K. The two elderly gentlemen folded, one with 7s 8s and the other Kh Qd. *This could take a while.* Steve scooped in the blinds and added them to his stack. He looked across at Dylan, who had about 50K. The dealer dealt the next hand. Steve didn't need to look at his cards, though, he could see Dylan had aces and the small blind, the smallest stack with 20K, had queens. Sure enough the action went all in, call, and it looked likely that they would go down to three. The flop was full of drama, though, the queens making a set on the Ks Qh Jc flop.

Dylan stayed remarkably calm, but thundered into life on the 10s turn. "Boom! It's my time, baby, it's my time!" The river was the 5s, and Dylan won the pot with a straight versus the elderly man's three of a kind. He flexed his biceps and shouted, "Nobody can match these guns!" His opponent shook hands with Steve and the other elderly gentleman, but made a point of not shaking Dylan's hand when he offered it.

Between them, Dylan and Steve ground the final player down, taking it in turns to raise. They hadn't agreed anything, but an understanding existed between them; it was the two of them against the other player. As the two big stacks, there was no reason for them to play any big pots against each other. Eventually, down to just 10K, the elderly bloke went all in with Ac 7h. Dylan called, with 6d 6h, and Steve decided just to call as well, with Kh 9s. The flop was 6s 5h 5c, giving Dylan a flopped full house. He and Steve both checked. The turn was the 4s, and it was Dylan's turn to act. He checked again, as Steve had expected, and Steve made an easy check behind.

The elderly gentleman sat up in his chair; an 8 or a 3 would give him a straight, and as far as he was aware, a 7 might give him the best hand. He was quickly disappointed on the 2s river, which again was checked by both Dylan and Steve. They all turned their cards face up, and the elderly gent couldn't believe Dylan had checked a full house all the way. For once it was Dylan's turn to be berated. "Why didn't you bet that?" he demanded. "Did you think he was going to do it for you?"

"Sorry buddy, but there was no point in me betting," said Dylan. "I don't need *his* chips…" He motioned towards Steve. "Only yours." The elderly man muttered under his breath before going to the registration desk to get his £120 prize. Dylan turned to Steve. "Congratulations buddy, you played well." Steve could hardly believe his ears. Firstly, Dylan was complimenting him, and secondly, he wasn't shouting.

"Ah thanks, mate. You did well too, especially to come back from being a short stack after you re-registered."

"Well, that's just the way I roll," drawled Dylan. "Dig out the win even when it seems like the world's against me." He smiled a very white smile at Steve. "Listen, I've got a meeting with the top brass here. If I don't see you, then good luck."

"Yeah, you too." Steve watched Dylan swagger off, trying to hide his surprise at his now calm and pleasant demeanour. *Maybe it is an act whilst he's playing, after all.* Steve made his way to the exit, smiling. He'd achieved the first stage of his plan, and it had been reasonably easy. He had his ticket to the main event, and was ready to finish this off once and for all.

* * *

Dylan Broadmoor walked into Eddie Liddell's office. The monitor was showing the table Dylan had just played on, and replaying hands. "So, what do you think?" asked Dylan, sitting down. "Is he cheating or just good?"

"He is one hundred per cent cheating," Eddie snapped. "I could show you loads of examples. He plays hand like 9-2 and beats people with ace queen, because he knows they haven't made a pair. And when they *have* made a hand, he magically knows to fold." He shook his head in disbelief, then turned a gimlet eye on Dylan. "Did *you* see him doing anything suspicious? How much did he touch his phone?"

Dylan shrugged. "He hardly touched his cell; I honestly don't think that's how he's doing it."

"Well, do you have any theories, then? I mean, you were sat with the guy for hours." Eddie said, with some venom.

"We need to watch him back on the tapes and see what he does," Dylan replied. "Does he play any other games in the casino?"

"No," said Eddie. "Just poker."

"Well, stick us both on the feature table on the first day of the event. Loads of people will be watching him, and they might see something we haven't. Keep your eye on the chat box Eddie, and note down anything that gives you a possible lead." Dylan got up.

"Good idea. Here's a couple of bullets in case you need extra for tomorrow. If not, keep it." Eddie reached behind his desk, held up a black rucksack that had once belonged to the Russian, and threw it to Dylan.

Dylan raised his eyebrows, unzipped the rucksack, took the money out, put it in his pocket and threw the bag back to Eddie. "Not sure you needed to bag it, dude."

Eddie scowled. "If you don't come up with anything more concrete, that will be the last money you get from us." He turned back to the monitor. "Work out what he's doing."

* * *

Steve went into the city centre for dinner, as a treat to himself for the day's work. He walked towards Nottingham castle and found a pub with white walls, that seemed to be built into the rock of a hill jutting into the sky. It looked cosy, a surprise considering he was in the city centre, and was called Ye Olde Trip to Jerusalem. Across the side of the wall in black paint were the words *1189AD, The oldest Inn in England. Bloody hell, it's 800 years old.* Steve walked into the bar area where he ordered a pint of Ghost Ship ale, before walking around the building looking for a table in the hidden alcoves. The deeper he went into the pub; the more Steve couldn't help but think he was venturing into the caves. Eventually he found a little room where he sat down, the wooden table wobbling as he rested on it. He ordered a steak, medium-rare and sat thinking about Dylan. He was an excellent player, and Steve wondered if he could take him on without the glasses. He'd love to be able to play like that. *It must be a thrill to know what your opponent's hole cards are without needing to cheat.* Then he grinned. *Well, I guess there's nothing to stop me reading some theory.*

Steve downloaded *Moorman's Book of Poker* and began reading through the hand histories within. *Holy shit, how do they even think of all this stuff while they're playing?* Steve couldn't believe how detailed and logical the thinking was. Most of his opponents wouldn't think this way tomorrow, on the first day, but they were more likely to the deeper into the tournament he went. *I'll have to be more careful where the decisions are marginal.*

Steve walked back through the city centre, which was buzzing with life. *Student city!* He reached the main road and headed up the hill towards his room. For a split second, he thought he saw the black SUV which had been outside his house. Then he shook his head. *There must be a million of them. Why would it be in Nottingham at the same time as me?* He smiled at himself. *Stop being paranoid, Steve.*

Steve continued uphill to the summit and looked down on the outskirts of the city. In the distance he could see the illuminated letters of Jacques Casino. He opened the door to the apartment block, and went up to his flat. Fifty metres away, a black SUV parked up at the side of the road.

Chapter 12

S teve woke feeling refreshed. The sun was shining through a crack in the curtains, and he had a good feeling about the day. He made some breakfast, Cheerio's and milk, and looked at his phone. Tanya had texted: *Hope you're behaving yourself and don't have too much of a sore head!* He finished his breakfast and called her. "Hey babe, how's it going?"

"Honestly?" said Tanya, her voice tight. "Terrible. Both the kids have got chickenpox." She paused. "How are you doing, did you have a good night?" Steve felt a pang of guilt. Here he was swanning around Nottingham, and Tanya at home on her own with two ill children.

"Ohh babe, I'm so sorry. Yeah, it's been ok. We just had a few beers yesterday, and we're going to play poker today.

"Oh, that's good." Tanya seemed slightly unsure.

"Can I speak to the girls?" Steve asked.

"Yes of course. They're in the living room. One second." A door opened with a squeal that would slot nicely into a horror movie. "Fiona, do you want to speak to Daddy?" Steve heard the phone fumbling between hands.

"Hi Daddy," piped Fiona. "Me and Ellie have got chicken pox and it really itches all on my body. But mummy says we can't scratch them, or the Pox Fairy will come and make them itch even more." Fiona sniffed.

"That's right," said Steve. "You mustn't wind up the Pox Fairy by scratching. Now, can you promise me you'll be good for Mummy, and give her some big hugs from me?"

"I will," said Fiona. "I'll give Mummy a big hug the next time she cries and tell her I love her."

"The next time she cries. Has Mummy been crying?" Steve asked.

"Yes, she cried after you left yesterday. I think she is missing you, and she's worried about not being able to pay a man called Bill. That's what she said to Grandad on the phone."

"I see," Steve said, feeling as if the stuffing had been knocked out of him.

"I love you, Daddy!" Fiona said cheerfully. Steve couldn't help but smile through the frown he'd been wearing.

"Can I speak to Ellie?" he asked.

"She's asleep," his daughter replied. "Shall I wake her up?"

"No, no, don't do that. Can you pass me back to Mummy instead?" Steve heard the phone being passed back.

"Hi." Tanya said, her voice flat.

"Hey babe, Fiona says you've been upset about the bills. I thought we were managing OK?"

"We were, until I got a letter from the nursing home. They're putting their fees up they want £4,000 per month. I've spoken to him and he's only got six months' worth of money left. After that, he'll have to be rehomed at the council home, it's like a prison in there." Tanya said deflated.

Steve felt anger rising inside him; but instead of trying to dampen it, he let it grow. "I'm going to make you a promise right now, Tanya," he said. "I'm coming back from this with the money to pay off our debts. We're not going to struggle anymore." Tanya didn't say anything, but down the phone Steve could hear the sniffles of a person trying not to cry.

"I love you, baby," she stammered between sniffs.

Steve gripped the phone tight. "I love you too."

* * *

Steve showered and got ready, his jaw set. He thought of all the things that had gone wrong since he'd left his job. By the time he had worked through them all, he was so fired up that he felt as if he could go ten rounds with Muhammad Ali.

Steve got in his car and drove to the casino. He was an hour early, so he registered for the tournament and then sat down at a table near the bar. The casino was already busy with people, but Steve sat at his table stony-faced for almost forty minutes. He jumped out of his chair when the seating chart flashed up on the screens, though. Once he'd found his table, Steve scanned the other names on the table. One name leapt out at him: Dylan Broadmoor. *What are the chances of that?* thought Steve. One by one he googled the other players. Some of them had won a lot of money at the WCOP in Vegas and were serious propositions. Others didn't return any results, and Steve made a note to target them.

The tannoy crackled, and an announcement blared out. "Our feature table today will be table seven. I repeat, table seven will be today's feature table. Smile for the cameras, players!"

Holy shit, thought Steve, *everyone will be able to see what I'm doing. I'll have to play like a normal poker player. Fuck, I haven't prepared for this...* Then Steve felt a hearty slap on his back. "Time for some tequila before we get started?" Grant said.

136

Steve snapped out of his bubble. He could feel the butterflies in his stomach, and they needed drowning.

"These are on me," he replied. They walked over to the emptying bar and drank two tequilas each, shuddering as the burning sensation spread through their chests.

Grant coughed. "Good luck, pal. Are we on for 10% again?"

"Of course we are. Good luck to you too mate." They each took their seats, Grant's in the standard chairs and Steve under the bright lights of the televised table.

* * *

Blake Andrew was tall and skinny, a shape incompatible with working in the small cupboard of a room otherwise known as the commentary booth. Nonetheless, he loved his job. He'd been interested in film and television all his life, and had even had his own late-night radio show with his local station Sun FM before getting the gig with Jacques Casinos. He was working with his usual partner Kevin Rawlings, who was an American E-sports commentator when he wasn't doing Poker commentary. They had now been streaming for eight years, growing their followers, so the process ran like clockwork.

Blake and Kevin each did mic checks, counting to two over and over before the sound engineer gave the thumbs-up. They each did some vocal warm-ups; then, when the countdown hit thirty seconds, they silently watched the lights in front of them, waiting for them to change. The *On-Air* light switched on above them. This was Blake's favourite part of the job, the tension before the start of a new stream. "Five … four … three…" The director counted the *two* and *one* on his fingers and Blake launched into his opening gambit.

"A very warm welcome to you all from Jacques Casino in Nottingham. My name's Blake Andrew, and I am joined by my favourite commentator after myself, Kevin Rawlings."

"What's happening, poker disciples?" said Kevin. "We are at the home of UK poker, the cathedral of Saints Flop, Turn and River, and I am excited for the weekend ahead. We always get a good turnout here in Nottingham for the True Grinder Series, and the casino floor is buzzing."

"It certainly is!" Blake agreed, as the shot on the screen flipped to the feature table where the players were taking their seats. "It looks like we're going to be watching the newly-sponsored pro Dylan Broadmoor, who has certainly got his fans – and also his haters – in the chat." Blake watched his screen as the messages in the chat box scrolled faster with people declaring their love or hate for Dylan.

"He is the Marmite of poker players," said Kevin, "but I've got to say I enjoy watching him play. "He knows how to talk people into feeling under pressure. In my mind Dylan Broadmoor is an old-school player rather than one of the internet whizz-kids, and as a fellow-American I'd consider it downright unpatriotic to support anyone else." Kevin's American accent twanged stronger as he spoke. "It's not often that we get to see any of the American pros on these shores, and I'm sure the British players down there will be looking forward to playing him."

"I'm sure they will," said Blake. "All right, it looks like the players are settled, and so we're going to hand you over to the tournament director Thomas Salisbury to introduce the tournament." The shot changed to that of a man in his mid-forties with a podgy face who looked a little bit lost. He was standing in the middle of the card room, dressed smartly in casino uniform, and holding a microphone.

"Ladies and gentlemen, thank you for attending the first day of the True Grinder Series Grand Final. The blinds will start at 100/200 with no ante, and levels will be thirty minutes. Dealers, please shuffle up and deal."

A sound like ripping paper filled the room as the dealers started shuffling their decks of cards. The shot on the screen switched back to an overhead view of the feature table, showing all nine players. The *click clack* of chips being broken into two towers and merged back together into one larger tower echoed through the room, and gentle chatter filled the air. Kevin leaned into his microphone. "So, Blake, what should we expect from these opening stages of the tournament?"

"Well, I'd expect we'll see most people playing small-ball poker, trying to feel each other out and work out the play," Blake replied. "There may be a few wild players out there who go big early to try and build up a big stack, but I imagine the majority will start off looking to play small pots." Play began, and he continued seamlessly. "OK, we're onto our first hand of the day and we see an open from Dylan Broadmoor to 300 from the cutoff position with Ace Queen of spades. It's been folded around to the big blind, Steve, who's sitting there with the ace of diamonds, jack of clubs"

Kevin took over from Blake. "This decision is a standard defend in the big blind spot, but Steve seems to be mulling his options over. Perhaps he is thinking about a three-bet, but it's early to start making moves, and definitely not something you'd want to do against Dylan." They both paused, waiting for Steve to make his decision.

"Well I hope we're not going to be waiting like this all day…" said Blake, to fill the silence. "Finally, we see Steve make the call and we're going to a flop of… Ace of clubs, ten of clubs, three of diamonds. No spades for Dylan, but he has the best of it. Steve quickly checks and we can see Dylan is now counting out some chips. He bets 250 and the action is back with Steve, who makes a quick fold!" Blake looked across at Kevin, eyebrows raised.

"Well, that is a great fold in this spot but definitely a losing play long-term," Kevin said, rather sternly. "There are all sorts of hands Dylan could have had, pocket pairs, king and another card, or a worse ace. Perhaps Steve has been watching Dylan on TV and has picked up on a tell."

"Either that, or he is nervous and misread his hand. We know he satellited in and have seen players who aren't used to the lights make strange decisions before." Blake added. It took half an hour before Steve was involved in another hand, and the commentators had almost forgotten about his first hand when he was dealt Qd Qh.

Blake's voice rose with excitement when the player to Steve's left, Phil, was dealt Jd Jh. "Well, we could see some fireworks going off in this hand. Steve has raised to 600 and the action is now on Phil. He raises himself, making it 1800 to go. The action is folded back around to Steve and it doesn't look like he needs any time to make his decision here. He's pulled a *big* stack of chips forward."

"4500," Steve said confidently to the dealer.

"I'd like to see a smaller four-bet here, or even a call," Kevin said, frowning. "I think with this sizing he will only put off players with worse hands, and get calls or raises from players with better hands."

"Well," said Blake, "it looks like Phil is going to make the call and we are going to the flop." He gasped. "Wow, what a flop! queen, jack, ten of spades, both players flop a set but there's plenty of straight and flush potential out there."

"THIS. JUST. GOT. INTERESTING!" Kevin boomed down the microphone.

"It looks like Steve is going to continue here. He bets 5000 into the already massive pot of 9200, and I don't think we should expect Phil to fold here either." Blake paused. "It's going to be tough for Steve when he sees at least a call here. His mind's going to be racing, wondering whether he's behind to a straight or a flush –"

"It is certainly going to work in Phil's favour here to have the positional advantage," added Kevin. "He does need some time to think about this one though, it could be a tournament-defining hand."

The camera zoomed in on Phil's face, the left corner of his mouth twitching upwards. He threw a chip into the pot. "Phil has made the call and we are through to a turn," said Blake. "Both players with just a pot-sized bet behind now. The three of diamonds doesn't change anything. Action on Steve now."

Both commentators paused whilst the camera slowly zoomed in on Steve's face. He was staring intently in Phil's direction, his eyes focused on the chips Phil had in front of him. Then he looked at the dealer before quietly announcing "All in."

The view switched to Phil, who was no longer trying to maintain a poker face. His face was contorted with the pain of his decision. Kevin could barely keep his excitement under wraps. "Steve Ash makes a seriously ballsy move here, and he's probably going to be rewarded with the pot. Whilst he clearly has the best hand, there are lots of potential things that could be beating him."

Blake cut in. "Now the decision is with Phil, who is going

through the same thought process Steve has probably just gone through. He might have the best hand with a set of jacks, he's beating hands like aces and kings, and Steve could be doing this with any hand that has the ace of spades. Even if he gets it in behind to a straight or a flush, he's going to have ten cards that can give him a better hand." He smiled. "The only hand he's really in trouble against is the exact hand Steve has, a set of queens, where he's only got the one jack in the deck left to hit."

"You can see the agony in his face," said Kevin. "This would be an amazing laydown if he can find the fold." Phil reluctantly threw a chip in and looked as if he might throw up when he saw Steve's cards. He stood up. "One time. Let me get there." The dealer waited to deal the river card, building the tension. Kevin, barely pausing for breath, stood up too. "Phil gets it in and sees the bad news. There's only one card left that can save him from crashing to the rail. His face, though, is the picture of a man who is already resigned to defeat." The dealer turned over the river card. "That's going to be the end of Phil Stevens's time at our feature table for now," said Kevin, as if pronouncing sentence. "The river was the six of clubs, not helping his cause at all. He's shaking the hands of all the players at the table. Wow, what a hand, and a huge double up for Steve Ash.

"His instincts certainly seem to be on point," said Blake. "Folding the ace jack earlier, then getting it in good with the queens. If he can maintain this form through the rest of the tournament, he could be a player to watch."

"It's still early days though, it can be lost as quickly as it can be won," warned Kevin, having calmed down from his earlier excitement. "On to the next hand!"

* * *

Steve reached the break with just over seventy thousand chips, winning a slightly smaller pot than he had with the queens just before the break. He searched for Grant and found him still playing a hand, deep in concentration. Steve stayed out of his line of sight so that he didn't distract him. Eventually Grant folded the hand, stood up and puffed out his cheeks. "Alright mate, how are you getting on?" Steve asked.

"Pfft, I've got a starting stack but it's a tough table," said Grant, shrugging. "They know how to put you under pressure at this level. I think I've folded a few more hands than I should have done." Grant glanced at Steve. "How about you? I was following you on the stream, but it was distracting me too much from my own game, so I had to switch it off."

"Yeah, good, mate, I'm up to 70K. I got lucky though, I had a cooler against a guy, my queens against his jacks," Steve said, missing out the detail of the straight and flush possibilities. They walked over to the bar and got a drink, then sat down. Then Steve saw Dylan striding towards him. He didn't sit down, towering over him. "You got lucky before with your queens, buddy," he spat. "Trust me, if you play a hand like that against me, I will shut you down. Go back to the low stakes tournaments where you belong." Before Steve could think of a reply, Dylan walked off.

"Fuck off back to the States, you Yankee prick!" Grant yelled after him. "What an arsehole," he said to Steve, who was still staring after Dylan. Why had he changed again? He'd been amicable at the end of the satellite, to the point where Steve had begun to think he might be able to make friends with a real pro. Then his shock turned into anger. *Who the hell is this guy to come over and tell me how to play? He knows nothing about me. The hand wasn't even against him!* Grant's voice interrupted his thoughts. "Don't let him get under your skin, mate. Try to forget about it."

"Yeah, I'll do that," Steve said unconvincingly.

Grant gave him a friendly pat on the arm. "You've got this, mate. You have the chips and you have the skills. If that doesn't work, you can always ask for a favour from Lady Luck." He smiled at Steve, who made an effort to pull himself together.

The tournament director called all players to return to their tables. Grant and Steve wished each other good luck, and they returned to their seats. Steve got back before Dylan and sat down, unsure what might happen. Dylan arrived at the very last moment and looked Steve in the eye as he took his seat. "Alright, buddy?" he said, as though their previous encounter hadn't happened.

Steve fumed in his seat. *How can he behave like this? I belong here more than he does.* The daydream he'd had the other day about beating Dylan in a pot flashed into his mind, and Steve took his glasses off, putting them into the case and leaving them behind his chips. *I'm going to win one hand, and then they go back on.*

* * *

Blake Andrews returned to the booth twenty-five minutes after the players had finished their break. The stream was broadcast on a thirty-minute delay so that players couldn't cheat by looking at the other players' cards on the stream. He'd used the time to walk around the card-room floor to soak up the atmosphere, avoiding the feature table so that he didn't spoil any of the action for himself.

Despite his best efforts, it had been impossible not to hear Dylan Broadmoor shouting at some poor soul. The only line he'd heard was, 'You're a fucking idiot'. He was looking forward to seeing what all the commotion was about, though he hoped Dylan wasn't being too hard on his victim. It wouldn't be a good look for the Jacques brand if he was name-calling other players. Still, he assumed the top brass at Jacques had known this would be a risk of sponsoring him. Blake hadn't had a say in who would be sponsored, but if he had, he'd have been firmly against Dylan. There were plenty of less controversial players who were amazing.

Blake and Kevin had different routines for their breaks. Kevin went to the bar for a Jack Daniels and a quick swipe session on Tinder. This was one of the reasons that Blake loved poker. He and Kevin were entirely different, yet this card game had brought them together and made them lifelong friends. He couldn't imagine doing the job without Kevin. He went through a quick vocal warm-up again before doing a test with the sound engineer. If nobody had touched the equipment this was usually straightforward, and today was no different. Blake settled into his seat with Kevin alongside, and they waited for the director of the stream to count down from five to one.

"Welcome back to Jacques Casino in Nottingham," said Blake. "We had a pretty electric opening two hours, and we have no reason to expect the next two to be any different." He could say that with confidence, since he knew it was all about to kick off in the next fifteen minutes.

"We certainly marked out some of the characters in the first session of play," said Kevin. "Dylan Broadmoor of course needs no introduction. The two-time WCOP Bracelet winner has built up a decent stack despite not really having any notable hands to play. He's sat there with fifty thousand chips. The chip leader of the table, though, is Steve Ash, sitting on seventy thousand chips. His instincts have been spot-on so far. He's taken his glasses off and I almost didn't recognise him without those big bulky frames." Kevin laughed. "Let's hope they aren't the source of his poker power." He checked the rest of the table. "There are some shorties playing too. Jeff Archer has ten big blinds, with just six thousand chips, and Jennifer Lowe, our first goth to make the feature table, has fifteen big blinds with nine thousand."

"They're going to be looking for double-ups pretty soon, before the blinds and antes force their hands," said Blake. "Now, the clock has started, and we're about to see our first hands dealt."

The dealer, a different one from the first session, expertly distributed the cards to the players. They looked at their cards in turn, aiming not to give away an intention to raise or fold before it was their turn to act; the sharper players would pick up on their body language. It was around seven minutes later when Blake saw Dylan open with the 4s 2s from the cutoff.

"Dylan Broadmoor is making an interesting play here raising with four two, but if the button folds, he's in position, and we know he's good at making moves." Kevin sat back.

"He certainly is," Blake replied. "Luckily for him the button folds, and so does the small blind. I've got to say it's quite a large raise as well, he's made it 3200 to go, almost four times the big blind. Well, action on Steve Ash now, and he has Jd 4d. Normally I'd say this is a fold, but he has a look in his eye." Blake leaned forward, studying him.

"He goes ahead and makes the call," Kevin reported. "Dylan looks a little irritated by that. The flop is the ace of clubs, ace of diamonds, six of clubs. Steve looks deep in thought, but I think the action will go check, Dylan bets, and Steve folds."

"Well, Steve *has* checked, so the action's with Dylan now." Blake settled in to watch.

Dylan suddenly burst into chatter. "Interesting that you call on your big blind, no matter what I raise. I don't think you have a single bit of that board, and I want to get as much from you as I can, so I'm going to let you catch up a bit."

Kevin was beaming behind the mic. "This has the potential to get interesting, Dylan is almost toying with Steve here, despite having the worst of it. He's checked back as well. The turn card is the eight of diamonds, which gives Steve the flush draw. He's checked a little quicker this time. I think he calls now if Dylan makes a bet."

"How much is in the pot?" Dylan exclaimed. The dealer, unable to answer, spread the chips across the felt so that Dylan could see their values. "Hmm, about eight thousand? Then I bet ten thousand!" Dylan picked up a tower of chips and slammed them down on the felt.

"Dylan over bets the pot!" exclaimed Blake. "Steve doesn't have the right pot odds to call for a flush, but we can see that he actually has the best hand. His face is rigid, he's concentrating really hard."

Steve threw the chips into the middle of the table. "OK, here we go, the river card is... a total brick. Three of hearts on the river, and action now with Steve. He's checked and we're back with Dylan."

"Dylan has got to bet here," said Kevin. "He can't go to showdown with four high, he's literally got the worst hand he could have."

"I'm all in" Dylan said, eyes wide and staring.

"Well, this would be an insta-fold for me in Steve's shoes," Kevin continued. "He hasn't folded yet, though… Could he make a call here?"

"It would be an amazing call if he did. I'm sure we'll be hearing from Dylan after the hand if he does make the call," Blake said, fully expecting Steve to make a miracle call.

"He still hasn't folded," said Kevin. "I'm not sure how long Dylan's going to be able to maintain his composure." He leaned forward. "Steve is reaching for chips… Ahh, he's putting his glasses on." He smiled. "This is going to be *so* disappointing if he's been sat there all this time thinking there's three diamonds out there." Steve frowned so much he looked as if he'd aged ten years.

"I call," Steve said. Dylan turned his cards over, and as Steve turned his, the entire table erupted in disbelief.

"WOW! That guy keeps his mojo in his glasses!" Kevin shouted down the mic.

"Steve Ash is on fire today! How on earth did he know he should call there? That's a huge moment in this guy's career; he won't forget this in a hurry, that's for sure."

Blake cut in. "Dylan seems to have taken it pretty well so far. He hasn't erupted yet."

Right on cue, Dylan lit up. "How do you *call*? *Jack high*? You are never good there with that hand. How do these people keep winning?" Dylan flung his hands in the air and stood up. "YOU'RE A FUCKING IDIOT!" he shouted; his face flushed with anger. He stormed away from the tournament area, but the rest of the players didn't notice; they were too busy congratulating Steve on a great call.

"How did you do it?" one of them asked.

"I don't know, I just had a feeling..." Steve said, unable to stop himself grinning. "I played a satellite with him to get here and he was bragging about how many bullets he was going to fire, so I figured he'd try and bluff a big pot against someone, and that someone was me."

* * *

Dylan strode down the corridor to Eddie Liddell's office. He was a little embarrassed about the hand he'd just played, but his overall plan had worked. He'd manage to rile Steve up enough to make a mistake, and he didn't even know it. He stopped outside a large glass office where he knocked on the door and knocked three times. Eddie shouted, "Come in," his deep voice sounding like a growl.

"It's the glasses," Dylan said, as soon as the door was closed behind him. "That's how he can see the cards." Eddie had the twitch stream open on one of the monitors in his office, and turned to watch it. "You're going to have to wait half an hour for it to catch up to what's just happened." Dylan said.

"Did you get knocked out?"

"Well, yeah. I've played with him over a few hours, but this was the first time he played without the glasses on. He didn't know what to do, then he put them on and made his decision almost instantly."

"I need to see the hand. It's good work though, Dylan, well done." Eddie got up and headed over to a drinks cabinet in the corner. "Do you want a whisky? I have Laphroaig or Glenfiddich."

"Got any Jack Daniels?" Dylan asked. Eddie raised an

eyebrow at Dylan before going to his office phone and ordering a JD on the rocks. "You don't know what you're missing, pal." He waved a hand. "Sit down; you don't need to stand to attention with me." His voice was unexpectedly kind, and Dylan couldn't help feeling suspicious; this guy didn't have a kind bone in his body. He hesitated, then took the seat on the opposite side of the desk. Eddie turned his monitor around so they could both see, and a waitress appeared at the door with Dylan's bourbon. Eddie motioned her over with a grunt and she placed a white napkin on the desk before putting the glass in front of Dylan.

Blake Andrew's voice cut through the silence. "Welcome back to Jacques Casino in Nottingham. We had a pretty electric opening two hours, and we have no reason to expect the next two to be any different."

"You seem nervous," said Eddie.

Dylan shifted in his seat. "Well, you're quite an intimidating guy."

Eddie barked a laugh. "Bloody hell, the great Dylan Broadmoor is scared of little old Eddie Liddell!" he said, chuckling to himself. "Dylan, as long as you don't fuck anything up, you have nothing to be worried about." He eyed Dylan. "Do you have a family?" Normally, Dylan supposed, people would feel uncomfortable answering this question. But he didn't, because he didn't have any.

Eddie turned a photograph around which was a picture of his wife, a glamourous lady who radiated confidence even through the photo and two grown up sons in their early twenties, muscles bulging through their tightly fitted suits. Their heads were shaved, and they looked mean, ready to snap at the slightest thing. "Those are my boys; that's Junior and that's Shaun," he said pointing to the two young men. They clearly worked out; the seams of their T-shirts were almost bursting under the pressure of muscle. "And this is the only woman in the world that can tell me what to do," Eddie said, pointing to the stylish woman standing beside his sons. Either she had looked after herself very well, or Eddie had married a lady at least ten years his junior. "They look lovely," Dylan said.

Kevin's voice interrupted their conversation. "Dylan Broadmoor is making an interesting play here raising with four two, but if the button folds, he's in position, and we know he's good at making moves."

"This is the hand," Dylan said, glad to be able to change the conversation. They watched the hand together, Eddie's eyebrows shooting up when Steve suddenly put his glasses on and followed up with an incredible hero call. Eddie stood up without saying a word, walked towards a portrait of Alexander Jacques, and grabbed hold of the frame, opening it outwards to reveal a safe. He punched in a code, opened the safe, and grabbed some bundles of cash, which he passed to Dylan. "Ten thousand, with thanks." He paused. "I'd appreciate it if we kept this to ourselves for now; I need to speak to my boss and decide our next steps. You should go and play the tournament again. There's a particularly good table with a load of fish on it; I'll fix you up with a seat."

"OK, thanks," said Dylan, bundling the money into his pocket and hurrying from the room.

* * *

Eddie stood at his window, looking out on the car park. Then he phoned Alexander Jacques. "He's got a magic pair of glasses that he's using to cheat. We know where he lives, so we can make the grab whenever you like. I assume he's going to get the usual?"

Alexander sighed down the phone. "I want to do something different. Any other game, I'd say rough him up and then get rid of him. But it's not the casino he's stealing from, it's the other players. I'm in Nottingham; I'll head over, and we can watch him on the stream and the cameras."

"If that's what you want to do, boss." The line went dead. Eddie turned away from the window and hung up. Dylan's untouched Jack Daniels sat on the desk. *What a waste,* he thought, before picking up the glass and drinking the liquid down in one.

* * *

"This is your last hand of the level before the break," Thomas Salisbury called through the speakers. Steve had an enormous stack in comparison to the rest of the players. They had given him a lot of respect following the call he had made against Dylan, and that had made it far easier to bluff them out of hands where they were marginally ahead or had missed a straight or flush draw. Players were starting to get short of chips, and had begun going all in.

This was Steve's favourite way of building chips. He had called a player when he held pocket fours, fully aware that they had gone all in with pocket threes. Fortunately, he had only run into one situation where he needed to call despite knowing he had the losing hand, calling a pair of aces with ace queen. The board had bricked out for Steve, but it hadn't really dented his stack. He had around 250K, the equivalent of slightly more than seven people's stacks. The blinds had really started to bite the players, and they were finishing on 800/1600 with a 1600 ante.

Steve looked towards Grant's table, but he wasn't there. He glanced over towards the bar and saw him sitting at one of the tables, nursing a beer. "How's it going, mate?" Steve asked.

Grant sighed. "No good, mate. Busted out ace king against a pair of queens, all in pre-flop. I hit an ace, but the guy made a set on the river." He made a face. "It's always harder to take when you get shafted on the river!" Then he brightened. "I can see you're crushing it, though. The commentators wouldn't shut up about a hero call you made against Dylan Broadmoor. What happened?"

"I called an all-in with jack high; he had a big stack as well. I played him in the satellite, so I knew he was bluffing." He shook his head. "I still can't quite believe I called it." His gut instinct before he'd put the glasses on had been that Dylan had nothing, but the temptation to check before making a decision had overwhelmed him. He couldn't believe quite how bad Dylan's cards had been. Yet even after he'd seen them it had crossed his mind to fold. *Most people wouldn't make this call*, he had thought. *I'm supposed to fit in.* Then he'd remembered that this was the last time he'd wear the glasses and he threw the chips in, happy to take the ensuing fanfare.

"Bloody hell, well done mate," Grant said. "Did you know he re-entered, and he's busted already?"

"No?" Steve said incredulously.

"Yeah, he got it all in with aces, but some guy called him with four six of clubs because he 'had a feeling', if you can believe it."

Steve howled with laughter. "That is hilarious! He was

153

bragging about how many bullets he had to fire, but I bet he wasn't expecting to use them like that!"

Grant couldn't help but join in. "Your face, mate, it's a picture," he said, chuckling.

"Ahh, it's just too much." Steve said, once he could speak again.

"Listen mate, I'll finish this beer and then make a move. I'll keep my eye on the stream, and best of luck." Grant said. Steve got a beer to keep him company, then returned to the table for the start of the third session.

They had been moved away from the feature table, much to Steve's relief; it had been taxing to maintain his façade under the spotlight. Steve decided to play occasionally until he'd recovered a little. He plugged in his earphones, and relaxed. The rest of the day was easy. Without the peering eye of the cameras Steve had been able to play his normal game and finished the fifteenth level on 600,000 chips. He was easily the chip leader of the tournament. The casino gave him a bank bag to put his chips in, *I hate this bit, how do you work this flipping thing?* He looked around as the players at this table undid the strip on the bag with ease having deposited their chips into the plastic and sealing it before writing in marker pen how many chips he had on the bag. *Why can't I get the fucking thing off?!*

"Do you want some help there dear?" a lady in her late sixties asked. She had crow's feet cracking through the makeup around her eyes but had a kind face and smile that warmed Steve's heart. *She looks like Tanya's mum did.* "Oh yes please. I don't usually get to this stage and I have no idea what I'm doing." Steve laughed.

"Don't worry about it dear." She said, picking Steve's chips up and throwing them into the bag. The number of chips

Steve had, made it an embarrassingly long encounter and by the time they had finished the rest of the players had vacated the tournament area. Steve looked around at a sea of tables covered in plastic bags as he left the cardroom, and he was gripped by a renewed sense of motivation at the end of an emotional rollercoaster of a day one. *You've beaten the TV table; you've got the chip lead, and no one suspects a thing. Keep going like this and there's nothing that can go wrong from here on in.*

Chapter 13

G rant drove home from the casino mulling the family situation over in his head. Rebecca had been getting gradually worse, falling over more frequently, and struggling to swallow her food. He didn't think it would be long before she'd need full-time care. Rebecca's work had been very good about the situation and had said they would continue to pay her in full until she died. After that, Grant would receive a death in service pay-out of five times Rebecca's salary. That would be about £450K, which would pay off the rest of the house and give them some money for a while, but it wouldn't sustain them in the long term. Grant did his best to keep his worry away from Rebecca. He wanted her to be relaxed and comfortable in her last few years, but in truth he had no idea how he was going to keep the family afloat.

He arrived back home to find Rebecca, Charlotte, Lola and Christina sat round the dining-room table. They had his poker chips and cards out, and seemed to be playing a game of their own. "What on earth is going on in here?" he asked, grinning.

"We wondered what all the fuss was about you playing this silly card game, so we thought we'd try it ourselves." Lola said, looking up at her dad.

"We quite like it!" Christina added. Never in a million years had Grant thought his family would be interested in playing the game, but he couldn't help but feel thrilled that they were having a go. A piece of paper with a list of hands written on it sat in the middle of the table. From the state of it, it had been consulted frequently.

"Who's winning?" Grant asked.

"I am!" Charlotte said happily. "Loser has to do the washing up; winner gets the last Mars bar in the cupboard!"

"Blimey, I didn't realise the stakes were so high!" Grant joked. "Is there room for another player?" He sat down, and they counted out some chips for him. Grant had felt disappointed about the tournament he'd just left, but in that moment, he totally forgot about his troubles.

Charlotte managed to win, although not without an intense heads-up battle against Lola, who wasn't ready to give up the win easily and Grant admired the competitor in her. Grant ended up doing the washing up, despite not having made any of the dishes dirty, because he'd given most of his chips away to his daughters. After they had finished, Grant paid Charlotte and he and Rebecca put the kids to bed.

Later, Grant and Rebecca sat on the living-room couch, arms wrapped around each other. "We're going to be all right, you know." Grant said, almost to himself.

"I know you will," said Rebecca. "I know it in my heart."

"Maybe I should try to get a proper job again." Grant said.

Rebecca sat up and looked him in the eye. "I don't think you should. I think you should keep studying and doing the stream. You're building a base, and I know how much you can make if you can get into the top group. I was researching it earlier!" They both laughed.

"Yeah, but what if I don't get to the top?" he said.

157

"You're Grant Johnson – you survived prison; you can do anything! Besides, you only get a few years on this earth. I know that better than most." She smiled. "You should try to spend as much of it as you can doing the things you love."

Grant looked at his wife with admiration, suddenly feeling inspired. *If you think that I can do it, then I'm going to put everything I can into making this a success. I'm going to do it for you.* He beamed as Rebecca laid her head on Grants chest, his head swimming with ideas about what to do with the doctor.

Chapter 14

B lake Andrew watched the director count down. "Welcome back to Jacques Casino, Nottingham, where we are approaching the money bubble. The players are taking their seats, and we have a new table to broadcast now we have lost our last Jacques Pro in the competition. We are going to focus on our amateur star from yesterday, Steve Ash. He's the chip leader on eight-hundred and twenty thousand chips, and he played extraordinarily well throughout yesterday."

"That's right, Blake," said Kevin, "I really enjoyed watching him play yesterday, and I'm hoping that we will see the same again from him today. What do you think we should be seeing from the big stack as we approach the bubble?"

"The best bubble players I've seen always know which players to target. They don't go crazy raising everyone, but instead pick the players who are trying to get into the money. I don't know about you Kevin, but I can't help but see Steve Ash as a poor lookalike for SpongeBob Square Pants with those glasses, do you think we should call him SpongeBob from here on?" replied Blake.

"I love it. The name Steve Ash is dead to us, we are now watching SpongeBob. Well we are going to get our first hand of the second session of day two underway," said Kevin, getting comfortable. "We have SpongeBob in middle position, and we're going to see him raise here with pocket jacks. He is going to make it twenty-six thousand to go. It's folded around to the big blind, who decides to let his hand go as well."

"That is exactly the type of play that I'm talking about," said Blake. "The big blind player only has fifteen big blinds, and he isn't looking to get his stack in unless he's got a premium hand."

"So, we move on to the next hand. It's folded around to SpongeBob again, who this time decides to open with ace of spades ten of hearts." Kevin grinned. "It certainly helps when you get the hands to raise with as well. Action now with Liam on the button with ace, jack of diamonds, and he decides to make a call."

Blake leaned in. "The blinds fold, and we are going to a flop." The dealer quickly placed the three cards face up in the centre of the table. "So, ace-ten against ace-jack… we see a flop of ace of clubs, seven of diamonds, and two of hearts, giving both players top pair. Action with SpongeBob again, and I'd be surprised if he folded to a continuation bet from Liam."

Kevin nodded in confirmation. "Yes, absolutely; he definitely shouldn't be giving up yet."

"We see him check, and Liam continues for twenty-seven thousand. SpongeBob quickly calls and we are off to the turn, which is the seven of spades pairing the board. SpongeBob here, thinking about his decision, and decides to check." said Blake, interested in how the hand was going to play out. "We can see Liam struggling a little with his decision. Although he has the top pair, it's perfectly possible that Steve could have called him on the flop with a seven. He doesn't want to bet again and get raised, and indeed he does check behind."

"I think this is a sensible move," said Kevin. "the king of hearts river means that these two players will split this pot if it goes to showdown. They both have two pairs, aces and sevens, with the king kicker. Steve might feel he can make a move here, though, and put some pressure on the medium stack."

Blake raised his eyebrows. "Well, that certainly is a large tower of chips he's pulling forward. Steve is going to make a bet here of 150,000. That is a pot-size bet and he clearly doesn't think Liam has a seven."

Kevin joined in. "I think it's probably safe to assume that a seven would continue betting on the turn. So, unless Liam has slow-played a full house or got there on the river, he might think this will get him off a chop pot."

"Liam is in absolute agony here," said Blake. "150,000 is about half his remaining stack; if he calls and loses, he will be absolutely crippled. He's holding his cards close to the line…"

Kevin let the moment hang. "…And there go the cards. Liam will be really disappointed when he watches this back in half an hour's time, but well played Steve 'SpongeBob' Ash. That's going to put him up to just over a million in chips, and he's certainly brought yesterday's instincts back with him today."

* * *

Steve really enjoyed playing the bubble and managed to gain another 300,000 over the course of half an hour. The play slowed as the tournament was asked to go hand for hand. They didn't play like that for long, though, a short stack going out with pocket queens versus pocket aces.

Steve, as usual, felt sorry for the bubble boy; the rest of the room applauded the fact that they had made the money, whilst he had to make a lonely walk to the exit. Steve couldn't help but let out a big smile, though. Part two of his mission was complete now he was in the money, and it was onto part three. The next stage was to get to the final table, and once they made it there it would be the end of the day. He would come back tomorrow with the hope of turning his life around and getting rid of the glasses once and for all. He just had to make it.

The day seemed to drag by, and Steve slowed down his own playmaking; he was comfortable with his stack and trying not to draw too much attention to himself. He restricted himself to playing hands he would have been happy to showdown whilst he had the cameras on him, and if his stack fell below 70 big blinds he would loosen up a bit to get it back over that mark. He kept replaying the conversation he'd had with his children in his head. He wanted to make it right with Tanya, and stop her from worrying about the debt and the bills. After several hours they were down to two tables, and the prize money for the players busting was starting to rise. As it stood, Steve was guaranteed to leave with £5000. He found himself adopting a ritual where, when he folded his cards, he tried not think about the game or why he was there, but instead zoned out. He didn't need to keep an eye on how the other players were doing; when he played against them, he could see exactly what they were trying to do.

The players who were left seemed to fall away one by one, until there were twelve remaining. Steve looked down at his hole cards, and two black kings looked back at him. Trying to hide his excitement, he reached for the black chips which represented 50,000, picked two up, and threw them into the middle of the table. It was only then that he looked over at the small blind and saw that he had pocket aces. *How am I going to play this? If there weren't all of these cameras around me, I'd just fold, but I can't do that, even on the flop, unless an ace comes.*

The player in the small blind looked at his cards. He did his best to hide his excitement, but Steve saw a little smile curl at corner of his mouth. He three-bet to 250,000, and the action was folded back to Steve. He paused, as if he had a decision to think about, but in truth he already knew what his plan was. He made the call and they went to a flop. The flop was Qh 7d 2s, about as dry a flop it was possible to get.

His opponent was first to act. *Please bet small, please bet small, please bet small!* His opponent bet 270,000, and Steve looked at his own chips. He had about 3 million, and this pot was already going to be a million if he called. He couldn't fold though, so he called.

The turn didn't help, the 3c seeming like a brick sent to taunt him. His opponent bet again, this time making it 500,000. Steve needed a miracle, but again he felt that a fold would look suspicious. Steve made the call. He shut his eyes. *Please ... one time.*

The poker gods heard his prayer, and the Kd appeared on the river. Three of a kind! Steve let out a pent-up breath. His opponent, confident, looked at Steve and announced "All in."

"Call!" Steve shouted, almost knocking the table over in his haste to turn his cards face-up. His opponent only had 700,000 chips left, but it didn't matter. Steve had managed to play the hand without being found out, and now he was in a strong position to go on and finish the job. It didn't take long for the final player to be knocked out after that, and as there were ten of them left, they were all at the final table.

Steve let out a huge sigh of relief as the plastic bags he had struggled with from the first day were handed out again. He looked at his phone and saw that he had a text from Grant: *Get in there, you jammy bastard!* Steve thought about calling Tanya, but as it was already past midnight, he didn't think she'd appreciate it. *I'll call her tomorrow morning.* He looked at the pay-outs from first place to tenth. Tenth place was guaranteed £7350, but his eye was on first place at a cool £64,325. *This is the reason I'm here,* he reminded himself. He looked around at the other players, recognising most of them. There were only one or two whom he hadn't played against but, based on the way they had played, most of them deserved to be there.

Happy that he had successfully bagged all his chips, Steve walked out of the casino, taking in the atmosphere and remembering the day when he'd gone to the casino in Luton angry. On that day, after he'd lost, he'd felt as if the lights were dim and everyone knew he was a total failure. This time the lights were almost blinding, and he walked with the swagger of a hero who had just saved the world.

* * *

Steve woke up early the following day to the sound of birdsong. He stretched in his bed, not yet ready to get up, and imagined the welcome he would get from Tanya. He didn't know whether she would be thrilled, relieved, excited … or whether it would just be enough to make her stop crying. He had dreamt all night about things that might go wrong. What if he had another hand like pocket kings versus pocket aces, or fate conspired to reveal his deception? He opened his eyes and looked at the white ceiling. *I can't wait for this to be over.*

On impulse Steve checked his email, and found one from three days ago, offering him an interview for an analyst's job.

He had been so caught up in winning the tournament that it was only now he'd thought to look. He typed a reply, saying that he was free most of the following week. He remembered the boredom of his previous analysis work; but after all that had happened, he was quite looking forward to leading a relatively boring life. He sent Tanya a text. *Hey baby, just thought I'd check in and see how you're getting on. I'm playing at the final table today and top prize is £60,000. All the boys are really excited. Told you I was going to win!* He signed the text off with an emoji winking.

Steve tried not to think about what the day had in store, and instead imagined himself as a tourist on the last day of his trip. He got dressed and went to a local cafe, where he ordered a full English breakfast and a large black coffee. He sat at the window table and watched the world go by. *I wonder how many people have ever tried to do anything like this. T*hen he smiled. *If they had, they'd never admit it.*

The tournament was due to start at one, so Steve went for his last walk around the city. It was a quiet Sunday morning, but it had been a busy night on the town. Empty beer bottles, chips and bits of kebab lined the pavement. After feeling like he'd approached his 10,000 steps for the day, Steve made his way back to the apartment. He gathered his belongings, and booked a taxi to the casino. As Steve walked in, he saw Alexander Jacques standing by the door to his office. He looked away and hurried past the man he had once struck a business deal with. He went to the bar, ordered himself a Diet Pepsi, and sat down to calm himself.

Gradually his opponents for the day came into the card room, the most striking of which was Jennifer Lowe. She wore a large black trench coat, with a dog collar around her neck with spikes sticking out from it. Her face was powdered white and her hair jet black. She had done her best to look as intimidating as she could. It was hard to tell how old she was, but Steve guessed she was still in her twenties. The players acknowledged each other but didn't engage in conversation. Poker could certainly be a social game, but when the stakes were this high it was important to keep your cool. Steve could not help feeling paranoid. His head darted around like a meerkat looking for predators. Then he glanced at his phone. Tanya had replied to his earlier message. In fact, she had sent a video. Steve pressed *Play*, and his two daughters, Fiona and Ellie, appeared, standing in front of the TV. "Good luck, Daddy!" they said in unison. "We know you can do it!" Steve closed the video and looked at Tanya's message below. *Whatever happens today, remember your three girls will always love you.* Steve felt himself relax, and when the tournament director called the players to the feature table, he walked over with the calmness of a man who didn't have a care in the world.

* * *

Blake Andrews walked into the commentary booth. It had been his home for the last two days, and truthfully, it had begun to smell. *I suppose that's what happens when you put three grown men in a small room for days at a time.* Kevin walked into the commentary booth a few moments after Blake. His face was pale, and he reeked of whisky. "For God's sake, Kevin, can't you lay off the booze for one night?" Blake snapped. Whilst they were good friends, spending this much time with the same person was bound to result in arguments.

"It's not my fault, Blake," Kevin croaked. "I went to the bar after we finished yesterday and some of the players wanted to buy me a drink. It would have been rude to say no."

Blake sighed. This was the one aspect of Kevin that Blake didn't like; his inability to draw a line between being sociable and being professional. "What time did you get back to the hotel last night?"

"Honestly, about one am," said Kevin, sitting down heavily in his chair and failing to meet Blake's eyes. *Yeah, right,* thought Blake, opening his bag. *Good job I came prepared.* He pulled out a tube of Berocca, some paracetamol, and a Red Bull, and handed them to Kevin.

"Don't ever say I haven't got your back." Kevin opened the Red Bull and took a hefty swig, belching gently as the carbon dioxide bubbled out of him, while Blake went through his usual routine of warming up his voice and sound checking with the sound engineer. Eventually Kevin joined in with the sound check and they watched the clock count down to the start of the day, Blake feeling the customary going-live butterflies in his stomach for what would be the final time that weekend.

"Hello, and a big welcome to all from Jacques Casino, Nottingham!" he cried. "This is Blake Andrews, and my favourite commentator after myself, Kevin Rawlings."

"Hello, my poker disciples, and welcome to the church of Saints Flop, Turn and River," said Kevin. "I don't know about you, Blake, but I am excited for this final table. We've been lucky to follow some of these characters all the way through from day one, and I'm gonna say this now, Steve 'SpongeBob' Ash is my bet for today's champion."

"He has certainly played well over the last two days," Blake agreed. "Some of the lay downs he has made have been incredible, some of the calls he has made have been even more impressive, and luck seems to be on his side." He shot a look at Kevin.

"Let's take a look at some of the other players who've made it this far. Jennifer Lowe is also one of the stories of the tournament; coming back from just four big blinds, she is now sitting third in chips and has looked good value for her position. She certainly isn't low anymore; in fact, if she wins, I'll pay her deed poll fee to change her name to Jennifer High." Kevin grinned, his usual good humour back.

"But we have some short stacks at the final table, too. Jordan Black and George Tambour both have less than ten big blinds." Blake said.

"Mmm." Kevin considered them. "It will be interesting to see whether they try to get themselves back into the tournament, or just try to ladder up and survive longer than the other short stack."

Blake watched the stream for a moment. "Well, the dealer is getting herself ready and the tournament director, Thomas Salisbury seems happy. So here we go with the first hand of today's final table for the Grand Final of the True Grinder series. The blinds are 9000/18,000 with an 18,000 ante, and we start with Jordan, who folds pocket threes, the action folding round to George Tambour who *also* has pocket threes." Blake let his surprise show.

"It seems George is giving this some thought with his short stack," Kevin commented. "It makes sense to go all in when you're on the button in this situation."

"Well, we do see George make the move with the threes, throwing all of his chips into the middle. Action with Jennifer Lowe now; she has king of diamonds, seven of clubs, but decides to let it go, and in the big blind we have Steve Ash who's got a pair of sixes."

Kevin grimaced. "This is an absolute sickener for George, whose two outs will have already been folded if Steve decides to call. He's going to need to make a straight or a flush. Steve is asking for a count, and he does make the call. So, George needs to see running spades or make a straight, both of which will be difficult." Kevin sounded pained on George's behalf.

"Look at the expression of disgust on George's face; he can't believe it," Blake said, with some sympathy. "The flop hasn't helped him very much; only one spade on the ace, jack, ten board. There is a *possibility* of a split pot here if a king and a queen follow on the turn and river." Blake said, trying to make the best of it.

"Oh boy, there comes the queen on the turn," said Kevin. "George has stood up, trying to eke out whatever extra equity he can."

"So, George Tambour needs a king to survive. I would imagine most of the people on the table are praying there isn't a king, so they can ladder up one position." Blake paused for breath. "Unfortunately, the river is a nine and George Tambour will be the first to leave our final table today." Secretly, Blake was happy that George had busted; he'd commentated on plenty of final tables where players simply never busted, and they tended to go on for hours and hours. Jennifer managed to gain chips and get to second place behind Steve. So far, they hadn't really played any hands together, until Steve found himself in position on her with Ac Ad. In a bizarre reversal of yesterday's hand, Jennifer had Kd Ks.

"Jennifer has found herself in a really tricky situation here; she has been three-bet by the chip leader and has pocket kings." Blake said. "She must think that she has the best hand, but she might not want to play a big pot out of position against the only player who could actually knock her out."

"Well she does go ahead and just call." Kevin laughed. "Her head must be spinning. There are far more hands that Steve could re-raise her with here that kings beat, and she may well think he's trying to bully her because of his position with the chips."

"The flop doesn't help her. The board is queen of hearts, jack of diamonds, seven of spades and there is certainly no reason for her to fold to one bet. She quickly checks and Steve has picked up his chips very quickly; he throws out a bet of 250,000 into the 360,000 pot." Blake pursed his lips. "Action back with Jennifer. She really doesn't look that happy with her hand; she keeps glancing at her own chips and looking at the chips in the pot, and now it looks like she's trying to watch Steve too."

"She does make the call, and it's the ten of clubs on the turn." Kevin thought. "This might actually be a good card for Jennifer if she can try not to fall in love with her hand. Ace king just made a straight, but it's hard for Steve to have that when she holds two of the kings in her hand. He could have three-bet ace queen which she is beating, but lots of the other hands that might have three-bet her here are going to be ahead now. Queens, jacks, tens – all beat Kings, with three of a kind, and so do aces, so it's possible that she might be able to find a fold here," Kevin explained.

"She checks again, and action is back with Steve. He might want to play this one cautiously too. The same range of hands that apply to Steve in Jennifer's position, apply to Jennifer from Steve's."

"Well it doesn't look like Steve is going to follow that line of thinking," said Kevin, "He's reached for his black chips worth 50,000 each. And that is a huge bet. He makes it 750,000 to call. I guess the only thing Jennifer might think, if she does believe she's beaten, is that she has an up-and-down straight draw. Any ace or any nine would give her the straight."

"Nope! she thinks she's beaten and lays it down. That is a great fold, in my opinion. I think Steve made it far too much on the turn; he's only ever really getting called by hands that beat him." Blake sounded slightly irritated.

* * *

Alexander Jacques and Eddie Liddell sat watching the stream in Eddie's office. The more they had watched Steve, the more convinced they were that he was using the glasses to see the cards. Alexander had still not decided what he wanted to do about the situation. His indecision had frustrated Eddie, although he had done his best not to show it in front of his boss. Had this been any other situation of a punter stealing from the casino, Eddie was sure that Alexander would let him get on with it, not wanting to get his hands dirty. In Eddie's mind, Steve was just as bad as the rest. It didn't matter to him that Steve wasn't stealing from the casino. He was a thief, and he deserved the same punishment as anyone else. *If anything, Steve's worse*, thought Eddie. *He's stealing from everyday people, not a casino that can afford it.* It made him angry every time he thought about it.

He had respect for Alexander, though. He'd grown up in a tough family and had become the CEO of the casinos despite his older brother wanting the position. Alexander had a level of grit and competitive spirit that could only come from being

171

the youngest of a set of brothers. He had met Alexander when they were both young, at the same boxing club, and when they had sparred together, they hadn't taken it easy. Eddie knew that Alexander had been a fighter, but old age and a taste for champagne had made him fat and slow. He had no doubt Alexander could still pack a powerful punch, but there was no way he'd ever beat Eddie in the ring now. Eddie had always made sure he'd kept his form. He never wanted to be caught in a situation where he couldn't defend himself.

Alexander had originally hired Eddie to work in the enforcement part of the drugs business. However, he had noticed Eddie's talent for detail, which made him useful within the casinos. Ironically, Eddie didn't care for gambling. He'd always taken his work seriously, though, and made it his business to understand the intricacies of all the games on offer. Poker had never really caused him any trouble, and yet here he sat with his boss and long-time friend, worrying that Alexander was about to open a can of worms he would never be able to shut.

They watched as players exited the tournament, and when there were five players left Eddie could hide his frustration no longer. "So, what are we going to do, boss? We can't keep letting this guy play if we know he's cheating. The longer we leave it, the harder it will be not to implicate ourselves in this mess. We need to end it."

Alexander leaned back in his chair. "Eddie, relax. We will sort this out, but I'm fascinated by the way he manipulates people. He doesn't seem to care about their emotions. You saw the way that Dylan reacted when he knocked him out, but he didn't bat an eyelid."

"That isn't true," said Eddie. "Dylan told me he'd gone out of his way to upset Steve in the break. That was what led him to make the mistake in the first place. He is too easily manipulated himself. The man's a pushover!"

"I understand your concerns, Eddie, but I want to see how this tournament plays out," Alexander said, with an air of finality.

"This is a mistake." Eddie said, twitching in his chair.

* * *

"We are back at Jacques Casino, Nottingham where we are down to our last three players," said Blake Andrew. "Steve Ash is our current chip leader with just over twelve million chips. In second place we have Jennifer Lowe who has eight million chips, and our third-place player with just two million is Jordan Black."

"Jordan has got to be happy with this result, though. He has managed to ladder his way up to at least third; and don't forget, he started the day as one of our short stacks." said Kevin, approvingly.

"He certainly should; the next place will play out just under £22,000. He's managed to gain just over £14,000 by choosing the right moments to go all in and to fold," Blake added.

"Well, it looks like Jennifer Lowe is going to get us started in the first hand after the dinner break; she raises from the button with king-nine of spades. Steve Ash folds eight-deuce in the small blind, and Jordan looks at his hand, but decides to throw his five three into the muck as well. So, Jennifer scoops the blinds." Kevin said.

The dealer gathered the cards in efficiently and started shuffling the pack. The familiar sound of chips clicking against each other filled the air; the players silent, focused on the task at hand.

"SpongeBob to get us underway this time," said Blake. "He raises with Ace, three of clubs. Jordan Black quickly folds his hand and Jennifer Lowe does the same." Blake tried not to sound too disappointed by the lack of action.

"Jordan Black on the button now with pocket sixes, and he could be thinking about shoving here," said Kevin.

"He is certainly giving it some thought," Blake replied. "And there we go. Jordan Black is all in for ten big blinds, and now we have Jennifer Lowe with ace-king of diamonds. It will be interesting to see whether she decides to flat call or whether she raises. She might raise to try and protect her hand from Steve, coming along for the ride."

"She raises to four and a half million, and SpongeBob quickly folds the queen-deuce off-suit. We're off to the races!" crowed Kevin. He paused, waiting for the dealer to deal the flop. "Jordan Black is still alive on that flop but it's certainly a precarious one – queen of diamonds, ten of spades, four of diamonds, giving Jennifer plenty of outs to hit. Any diamond will give her a flush, any jack will give her a straight, and of course she can still hit an ace or a king to make a bigger pair."

"The turn is the six of clubs," said Blake. "That's a great card for Jordan, he now has three of a kind, but he still has a lot to dodge. Any diamond and any jack will still give Jennifer the best hand, but they cannot pair the board, otherwise Jordan will have a full house. This could be a huge card for Jordan; he's been a short stack for such a long time." The river card was dealt and there were a combination of groans and cheers from the rail as the Jd hit the felt, giving Jennifer a straight over Jordan's trips. Jordan was very gracious in defeat, congratulating Jennifer on winning the hand. He made a point of shaking Steve's hand as well, before leaving the tournament area to collect his £22,750 winnings.

Steve breathed a huge sigh of relief. Whatever happened, he was guaranteed to walk away with at least forty thousand pounds in his pocket. *I've done it.* Of course, he still had the potential to make another twenty grand, but this was more than enough to pay off his debt. He allowed a broad grin to spread across his face and congratulated Jennifer, a smile breaking through her façade, on making it to the final two. She thanked him, then said something that almost knocked him off his feet.

"Would you consider a deal?" She smiled at his expression. "I've got to say you played extraordinarily well. I've been watching you on the stream throughout the tournament, and I'm sure you'd make a great adversary in a heads-up battle. But I've played plenty of these types of tournaments before and I know how wide the variance can be when you get to the final two." She paused to let that sink in. "As we are both even in chips, more or less, why don't we split the money fifty-fifty?" She continued to smile at Steve; she seemed confident of a *yes*. It crossed Steve's mind to say no. He could see what cards Jennifer had – obviously, she didn't know that – but it seemed like a big advantage to give up. Steve was sure that most people in his situation would say no. But he'd achieved what he set out to do. They could play on now, and he might well win the first prize; but things could easily go wrong too, as they had the last time, he'd been heads-up. Jennifer might just get better cards than him and hit pairs or better. He could risk that; or he could agree to walk away now with an extra twelve grand in his pocket, on top of the forty he was guaranteed to win.

He took a deep breath. "Do you know what, I'm not gonna be

one of those guys who gets too greedy, so let's do a deal. I'd be happy to shake your hand on an even split. Let's take £52,000 each, and run one hand to see who takes the trophy." Steve offered his hand, Jennifer shook it firmly, and the tournament director asked them both to sign off that they were happy with the deal. Suddenly, Steve felt very tired. He couldn't wait to get home and see Tanya and the girls. His mission was over, and it was time to return to normal life.

They ran the final hand, and Steve ran out the winner with three of a kind on the river. Blake Andrews left the commentary booth to present the trophy to Steve, congratulating him and letting him know about the new nickname he'd been given. *I've been called worse.* He posed for photos with the trophy, a large glass vase, almost the same size as Steve's upper body, with 'Steve Ash: True Grinder' engraved into it and his winning hand, which he was slightly embarrassed about, as it was seven-two off-suit. Once they had finished taking photos, Steve walked over to the cash desk and was greeted by a lady in her forties who had massive bags under her eyes. She looked like she'd been awake for three days.

"Well done love, I'll bet you're well chuffed with your winnings." a grizzled voice droned from behind the glass screen. "How would you like to get your prize?"

"Can you send it through on a bank transfer?" Steve asked.

"Yes dear, I'll need your account number and sort code please." Steve gave her his details and she input them into her computer, her long nails clacking against the keyboard as she typed. "Shouldn't be long now love, I've got the blue spinning wheel going on the screen... So, you going to do anything nice with the money?" *How nosey is she?*

"I haven't decided yet, I'll probably put it into some savings."

"You could go on a nice holiday somewhere, maybe try the Greek islands if you haven't been? I went last year, they've got some lovely... Ooh, your transfer's just gone through. Here's your receipt love. The money should be with you in the next two hours or so. Anything else I can do for you?"

"No that's it thanks!" Steve said as he grabbed his receipt and got out as fast as he could. He made his way back to the Astra and put the trophy in the passenger seat, strapping it in with the seat belt. He drove back to the apartment, where he had planned to stay at for one more night, but instead he packed his bags and headed back home.

Chapter 15

Steve decided to wait until he got home to tell Tanya the good news. A weight had lifted from him; a weight he hadn't even known was there. As he drove, he couldn't stop smiling, even when his cheeks began to ache. He couldn't believe he'd managed to pull off the heist and get away with the money, and he couldn't help but laugh at the audaciousness of what he'd achieved.

Steve put on his favourite rock playlist and sang at the top of his lungs all the way home. It was around 9 pm when he got in, and the lights were on in the living room. Steve let himself in and walked into the sitting-room to see Tanya open-mouthed on the sofa. "I wasn't expecting to see you today," she said, patting the seat beside her. "How come you're back early?"

"Well, baby, you know that tournament I said I was going to win?" said Steve, savouring the moment. "I only bloody went and won it!"

"Are you having me on?" Tanya said, jumping out of her seat. Steve whipped out his phone and showed Tanya the balance of his online bank account, in which sat an additional £52,000. Tanya didn't say anything. She simply stood there, unable to stop herself from shaking, tears streaming down her face. Then she stepped forward and hugged him, whispering "I love you, baby," into his ear.

"Um, I should probably bring my stuff in," said Steve, disengaging himself gently. He fetched his suitcase, took it up to the bedroom, and began unpacking. Tanya stood in the bedroom doorway; a broad grin spread across her face.

"Why don't you go and get yourself a beer? You deserve to celebrate. I'll unpack your bag and put your dirty stuff in the washing machine."

"Thanks babe, you're the best!" Steve said, unable to suppress a yawn. He went downstairs, got a beer from the fridge, and went to watch TV. He heard Tanya come down, and the clunk of the washing machine door opening. *You star*, he thought. Then he remembered the trophy, still sitting in the passenger seat of his car. *I must show Tanya that,* he thought, getting up.

He walked into the kitchen holding the trophy above his head with both hands; then nearly dropped it when he clapped eyes on Tanya. She was wearing the glasses. "I-I can explain," he stammered, putting the trophy on the worktop. Tanya whipped the glasses off and stared at him.

"You'll need to. Even I can tell that these aren't normal glasses. Why do they say *Loading*? Loading what?"

"Things were desperate," he whispered. Tanya continued to look at him, waiting. "I just needed to find a way to get us out of the mess that I got us into. I never meant to hurt anyone, I never meant for anyone to find out. I can't believe I was stupid enough to bring them back from Nottingham. But please know I always did it with you and the girls in mind. It was never for me. I just wanted to repair the damage I'd done."

"So, this is how you won the tournament," said Tanya. "By cheating."

Steve looked at the floor. "Um, yeah."

She sighed. "What exactly do they do?"

Steve looked up, expecting to see fury, but Tanya looked strangely calm. "They're a miniature version of the cameras that James and I installed in the casino. I've been using them to see the other players' cards."

Tanya turned away, and Steve's heart sank. *I've lost her.* Then her shoulders relaxed, and Steve felt a glimmer of hope. Then she faced him, still with that calm expression. "I really don't know how I should feel. You've done something really bad, Steve, but you did it for the right reasons."

Steve took a step towards her, but she held up a hand. "Are you sure nobody knows you did this?"

"Yes, I'm certain." he replied. "They'd never have let me take the money if they'd caught on."

"You can never, ever use these again," Tanya said. "Do you understand?" She sounded as if she was admonishing one of the children. Steve swallowed. His mouth was bone dry.

"Yes."

Tanya sighed, and her shoulders drooped, as if the fight had gone out of her. "Go out and get rid of them. Somewhere that can't be traced back here. When you come back, we'll talk some more."

Steve opened the front door a crack and looked outside. It had begun to rain, so he grabbed his raincoat before leaving. He knew exactly where he was going to get rid of them, and set off at a fast walk. He crossed the road, taking a shortcut down an alley, then took a sharp left and followed the road around a block of flats until he reached the canal bridge. He stood at the top of the bridge and opened the glasses case one last time. He looked down at the nerdy frames, smiling at what he'd got away with. *Never again.*

"Ow!" Steve clapped a hand to his neck and felt something small and sharp lodged there. *What the fuck?* He pulled it out. *A dart...*

And everything went black.

Chapter 16

Steve woke up, stiff and cramped. He opened his eyes to red light. *Where am I?* He tried to uncurl himself but couldn't. His hands and feet had been tied together, and he was gagged with a strip of cloth. But he was moving; he could feel his body pushing against the space he was in as he changed direction, and he could hear the hum of an engine. *I'm tied up in the boot of someone's car. What the fuck is going on?* Steve wriggled around testing what he could and couldn't move. Whoever had kidnapped him had tied him up expertly, and there was no give in the knots. He tried to remain calm; there was nothing he could do. He couldn't even hear any passing traffic, only occasional birdsong when they came to a halt. Eventually, they stopped, and he heard the clicking of a handbrake. They had reached their destination.

Steve braced himself for a fight, and as the boot was opened, he wriggled around trying to resist his captor. His captor looked muscular and wore a black hoody with the hood up covering his face in shadow. He grabbed Steve's shoulder, and punched him hard in the face, a white fist flashing out of the black sleeve. Then he dragged Steve out of the boot, and Steve glimpsed what looked like the car park of an industrial estate before a black bag was thrown over his head. It smelt of dog. "This will all be over soon." a voice with a thick eastern European accent told him. *What the fuck does that mean? Are they going to let me go, or are they going to kill me?* Steve thought about Tanya, and the way that they had left things. He wished it could have been different. He thought of his two young daughters and prayed he would get the opportunity to see them again.

He was pulled into a cold building, the door making a loud metallic bang as it was closed. Then he was dragged across a large concrete floor, before being sat in a chair. He tested his bonds, trying to escape, and received another hard punch to the gut, knocking the breath out of him. The Russian kicked his legs out from underneath him, and Steve landed hard on a chair. The Russian pulled his arms around the back of the chair, tying them together whilst Steve tried to catch his breath, before wrapping some rope around his midriff. Steve felt the rope pulled tighter, his raincoat protecting him from rope burn. He removed the bag on his head and the binding in his mouth and eventually Steve caught his breath, but it was too late, he had already been tied to the chair. The man walked away and out of the metal door he had come through. Steve stared straight ahead, at a man sitting across from him, also tied up. He had been beaten unconscious; he had two swollen black eyes, and his face was so covered in cuts and bruises that Steve barely recognised him. "James…?" he whispered. He heard the metal clang as the Russian left the building.

James didn't stir. "James, wake up," said Steve in his normal voice. "It's me. Steve." James stirred and opened one eye; the other was swollen shut. The eye fixed on Steve.

"Uh."

"What the hell is going on?" Steve asked.

183

"Huh, Stevey-boy. Didn't think I'd see you again." He spoke slowly, his mouth struggling to form words. "I know why I'm here, but I don't know about you." Bloody spittle trickled from the corner of his mouth.

"Why did you do it, James? We could have had a great business together, but you double-crossed me and left me with crippling debt. I nearly lost everything." Steve's voice rose.

"Sorry 'bout that…"

Steve stared at James. "Is that all you can say?"

James shrugged as best he could. "What do you want me to say? Do I regret it? No. I made so much money, I tasted real power, and you've got to climb over people to reach the top." He spat some blood onto the floor. Steve's eyes widened. Even now, when they were probably both about to die, James regretted nothing. And it was James' fault that he was here. Steve looked around the warehouse. *Is there anything here I could use to escape?* There was nothing in his line of sight. He tried to move the chair, using his hips to propel himself forwards. He managed to move a few inches, but not without making a loud scraping noise. "Heeeeeelp," Steve yelled, at the top of his lungs.

James looked up at him with his one good eye. "Don't waste your breath pal," he said. "We're in the middle of nowhere." Steve heard a loud metal clang behind him. He wriggled in his chair, trying to break free. He turned his head round as far as he could, still shouting for help, and eventually a short, muscular man walked into view. He motioned to Steve for silence, and Steve closed his mouth.

"The famous Steve Ash," he said, smiling. "I've been watching you for a long time." Steve stared at him. *They knew all along.* "You're probably wondering who I am; my name is Eddie. I'd shake your hand, but you seem to be a little tied up," he said, the smile becoming a smirk. "I believe the two of you have already met," Eddie said, indicating James. "In fact, if my sources are correct, we're not the first people James has screwed. The two of you had a business together, right?"

Eddie walked out of sight, and Steve heard the sound of running water. Then Eddie reappeared, holding a bucket. "Let's wake you up a bit," he said, and taking careful aim, threw the bucket of water over James. James gasped for breath, then shivered violently, looking up at Eddie with his one eye.

"How does this make you feel, Steve? Seeing the man who stole your life like this?" He put on a knuckleduster, then punched James in the face. As he made contact, Steve heard the crunch of breaking bone. "This is for Steve, you prick!" he yelled. Steve closed his eyes. He hated James, but he couldn't watch this. "Oh no, no, no," Eddie said, very reasonably. "You can't close your eyes, Steve, you'll miss the show." Steve reluctantly opened his eyes. To his relief James was unconscious again, his head lolling on his chest.

Eddie walked over to Steve and crouched, so that they were eye-to-eye. "You've been a naughty boy too, haven't you Steve?" he said, in a sing-song voice. "You've been using technology to cheat, haven't you Steve? You've won a lot of money, haven't you Steve?" His voice grew louder with each question. "Have you seen the movies where people get caught cheating in casinos? Have you seen what happens to them? People don't think that happens in real life, and they're right." He leaned in until his face was very close to Steve's. "We're far worse," he whispered, and a maniacal smile spread over his face.

Eddie straightened up and walked back towards James. "Our friend James here got greedy. Did you know we were using the cards on the blackjack table too, Steve? Now, there are only a few people with access to the video feeds. Myself, the casino managers, and James fucking Baldwin." He punched James hard in the gut, and James regained consciousness, groaning and hunching over as far as his bindings would allow. He coughed as he tried to catch his breath. "James decided he was going to use his inside knowledge, just like you, except he couldn't do it himself. So, he sent some little rats in to do it for him. They sat at our blackjack table, while James here fed them information through a tiny earpiece. They stole hundreds of thousands of pounds," he said, his lip curling. "We brought one of them in for interrogation, and when we offered to let him keep some of the cash, he spoke up pretty quick." Bloody drool started to dribble from James's mouth again.

Eddie walked back towards Steve. "Now then, Steve, you like games, so I'm going to play a little game with you. Don't worry, the rules are very simple. I'm just going to ask you some questions. Every time you answer with a lie, I'm going to punch you... and if you answer more than one question in a row incorrectly, I'm going to hit James with that baseball bat." Eddie pointed to a spot almost out of Steve's peripheral vision. "I'll just move it a bit closer." Eddie walked away and returned, scraping the bat along the ground as he walked along. When he got back to Steve, he dropped the bat with a clatter which echoed around the room.

"Let's start with an easy one," he said. He crouched down suddenly, and Steve flinched. "Did you cheat at poker?" Steve thought about whether he could lie, then realised that even if he had played legitimately, Eddie had decided what the correct answer would be.

"Yes, I did," he said reluctantly. James's head lifted slightly at his admission of guilt. Even through the bruising and swelling of James's face, Steve could see his surprise.

"Good man. I hate it when people lie," said Eddie. "Next question. Did you use these glasses to do it?"

Steve looked up to see Eddie holding his glasses. "Yes, I did."

"Good; you know how to play." Eddie walked out of Steve's eyeline and Steve heard a dragging sound. When he came back into view, he was pulling a small table, which he positioned in front of Steve. "Look down." On top of the table were pictures of Tanya, Ellie and Fiona. *Shit, shit, shit. How the fuck does he know that?* Steve gulped. *I can't give them up.* "Is this your family?" Eddie asked, a searing tone in his voice.

"No, I don't know who they are." Eddie tilted his head from side to side, cracking the bones in it, before hitting Steve in the stomach with as much force as he could muster. The air left Steve's body like a balloon deflating, and he gasped as he tried to catch his breath.

"Let's try again." Eddie paused. "Is this your family?"

Steve, still gasping, looked at Eddie, then at the floor, and shook his head. "I don't know who they are." Eddie leaned down, picked up the baseball bat, and walked over to James.

"I didn't want to do this, but Steve is making me." He drew the bat back to his left ear, then swung it, making a sickening impact with James's chest. The sound of breaking bone filled the room. The chair clattered against the cold concrete floor as James toppled backwards with the force of the blow. He groaned, and choked on his own blood. "Is … this … your … family?" Eddie shouted.

Steve looked at the floor, his whole body shaking, "Yes."

"Fucking hell, that was hard work," Eddie growled. "I've told you not to lie, Steve!"

187

"I'll do whatever you want me to do!" Steve cried. "Please don't hurt my family. I'll give you back the money – you can even kill me – but please don't hurt them!"

"Oh no," said Eddie. "We don't want your money or your family, pretty as they are. My boss, in his infinite wisdom, has decided that what he wants is for you to continue cheating in the casino." Steve stared at him. *Have I gone mad? Am I hallucinating?* "You see," said Eddie, leaning on the baseball bat, "Poker is the only game that isn't rigged in the favour of the house. Your glasses, though, give us the opportunity to do just that." He grinned. "You're a lucky boy, Steve. If it were up to me, you'd be in the same state as him." Eddie pointed towards James. "Do you understand what I'm saying, Steve? You will play tournaments for us, we will pay your entry, and you will win. Second place won't cut it. You'll run errands for us, and you will *not* ask any questions." Steve flinched as flecks of spittle hit his face. "If you don't play, we kill your family. If you get caught, we kill your family. If you go to the police – which I wouldn't advise as we own them too – we kill your family." He leaned even closer. "Have I made myself clear?"

"Yes," whispered Steve. "I understand."

"Good." Eddie stood up. "Here's your first job. Get rid of the body." He pulled a Beretta M9A3–silencer attached–from under his jacket, walked over to James and held the gun at arms' length, aiming at James' head. Then he squeezed the trigger. Eddie walked behind Steve and cut him free. For a fleeting moment Steve thought about attacking Eddie. But before he could come up with anything, the door had clanged shut. Eddie would be long gone by the time he reached the door. Steve glanced at James's body. Blood was oozing onto the floor around him. Steve clapped a hand to his mouth, jumped up, and got a couple of steps away before vomiting violently. Retching, gasping, he looked back at the body. *How the fuck am I going to do this?*

He looked around the building to see if there was anything he could use to dispose of the body. There were some barrels in the corner of the warehouse, and he walked over to investigate. They were full of dark, thick liquid. *Oil?* Steve tipped the barrel onto its side and rolled it over towards James. It was only when he was halfway there that he noticed the barrel had punctured, leaving a thin stream of oil which led back almost to the other barrels. He rolled it next to James, opened the seal, and winced as the oil glugged out over James's lifeless body. *I'm sorry, mate,* he thought, looking away.

Now he needed something to create a spark. There was nothing obvious, and Steve stood for a while, wondering what to do. The warehouse was almost empty. Maybe there would be a canal or river nearby where he could dump the body. He opened the door and looked out to see a black SUV, parked facing the door. The headlights flashed, and the car drove towards him. It stopped with the driver's side facing him. The window lowered, and the Russian asked, "Is the job done?"

"No," said Steve. "I need to find something to make a spark."

The Russian shrugged. "I sit in car and wait for you to complete job." The window glided up, and the car drove back to its spot. *Thanks for nothing,* thought Steve. *Bet you do this kind of thing all the time.* He walked back into the warehouse, idly kicking a rock which clanged as it hit the side of the building. *I wonder...* Steve picked up the rock, took it to the pool of oil, and scraped it quickly along the concrete floor. Nothing. *Come on, you fucker.* Feeling stupid, Steve looked around the warehouse again. *One more try.* As fast as he could, Steve dashed the rock against the smooth floor. A spark flew and drifted lazily towards the oil. A flame licked up, then began to spread, first moving slowly, then gaining pace until it rushed towards the barrels. Steve's smile became a rictus of panic. He ran for the door, slamming it shut behind him, then sprinted towards the black SUV, waving his arms frantically. The car didn't move. An almighty explosion blew Steve forward, the fire lighting up the night sky behind him.

He looked up from the tarmac, and the SUV was beside him. The passenger-side door opened. "Pridurok! English moron get in car now!!" the Russian spat, as Steve clambered in. The wheels squealed as the Russian put his foot to the floor.

Epilogue

Tanya had given it two hours before deciding to go out and look for Steve herself. She had tried to call his mobile, but had been frustrated to find it by the windowsill near the stairs. She woke the kids up. "Fiona, Ellie, can you get dressed and come with mummy please?" She walked over to the Bensons house and knocked on the door. Leslie Benson answered the door, a buxom lady who had always been very friendly to the Ash's. "Leslie, I'm really sorry to do this but would I be able to leave Ellie and Fiona with you? Steve was meant to pop out for ten minutes and that was two hours ago. I'm worried something might have happened to him."

"Of course, I'll make some beds up for them. Take as long as you need love." She walked the streets, in the driving rain, but there was no sign of him anywhere. When Tanya got back to the house, she realised that the Astra was still on the drive. *Now I'm really worried.* She let herself in, took out her phone, and typed *'How to report a missing person'* into Google. The questions she would have to answer flashed onto her screen. *Is the person at risk? I don't know...*

She dialled 101. "Hi, I'm calling to report a missing person. My husband went out for a walk two and a half hours ago, and he hasn't come back." She paused for breath. "He was only meant to be out for ten minutes –"

"OK," cut in the operator. "I'm going to open a record as I can hear your concern, but you should know that standard procedure is not to deploy policemen until the person has been missing for more than twenty-four hours unless they are considered to be at risk."

"OK," Tanya replied.

"So firstly, what is the name of the person missing?"

"Steve Ash," said Tanya.

"Does Steve suffer from any physical or mental health issues, suffer from Alzheimer's or any other form of dementia, or have a drug or alcohol dependency?"

"No." Tanya replied.

"Does Steve have any medication or care required on a regular basis?"

"No." Tanya repeated.

"Has Steve been acting out of character, or been under stress recently?" *You mean apart from losing his business, barely scraping by financially and resorting to stealing money in a casino to pay the bills?*

"No."

"OK, so according to our criteria, he is not at risk." The operator paused. "What I'll do now is take some more details from you, and we will call back twenty-four hours from now. If he hasn't returned home by then, we will despatch officers to your address to do a routine search."

Once the call had ended Tanya could do nothing but sit by the window and wait for Steve to return. She stayed awake most of the night, but eventually, overwhelmed by exhaustion, she fell asleep on the sofa. Tanya was woken by the click of the front door closing. She shuffled into the hallway, still half-asleep. "Where have you been?" she asked; then her eyes widened at the sight of Steve. His face was badly bruised and cut, and he reeked of smoke.

Steve met Tanya's eyes, then sank to his knees. "Home," he whispered, and curled into a ball, hugging his knees. Tanya crouched down beside Steve and stroked his hair.

"What happened to you?"

Steve looked past Tanya, his expression vacant. "The casino. They kidnapped me, they killed James, and they made me get rid of the body. They want me to play poker for them, and I can't say no." His voice was flat, dull.

"They killed James. Why was *he* there?" Tanya cried. "None of this makes sense!"

Steve looked up at her, a deep sadness in his eyes. "They had pictures of you and the kids. They threatened to kill you all if I didn't do exactly as they said."

"Oh, fuck." Tanya said, unable to believe her ears. "What happened after you left the house with the glasses?"

"I went to the canal bridge to throw the glasses away, but they already knew I was cheating, and how. This Russian guy shot me with a tranquiliser, and I woke up in the boot of his car. They dragged me into a warehouse and tied me to a chair, and James was there. They laid into him and made me watch..." Steve retched, and his whole body stiffened.

"Oh, baby..." Tanya lay down beside him and wrapped her arms tightly round his shivering body.

"They showed me some pictures of you, Ellie and Fiona," Steve choked out. "They said if I don't play for them, they'll kill you all. And they'll do the same if I get caught, or if I go to the police."

Tanya shivered too. "So, what happens now?"

"They said I should lay low and await further instructions." Tanya had no idea what to do, except to continue holding on to Steve. They lay there, curled together, until Tanya's wake-up alarm rang on her phone.

"Listen, you're still alive, I'm still alive and the kids don't know any different. When we got married, we agreed to stay together until death do us part. Well death hasn't come to either of us yet, so whatever trials we have ahead of us, we will get through it together like we always do, and we will find a way out of this. I've got your back Steve, like you've had mine. Come on, let's move to the sofa," Steve got up from the floor and followed her into the front room. He sat down, face still vacant.

Tanya went into the kitchen and made them both a cup of tea. When she returned, Steve had turned on the TV. "We're bringing you live pictures of an explosion at a warehouse near Leicester," the reporter said. "The fire service has just about got the fire under control, but it is thought that the fire may have been caused by arsonists. We'll bring you more details as we have them."

Thanks For Reading

I hope you enjoyed reading This is Where You Fold. Why not pick up the next book in the series, This is Where You Call, today?

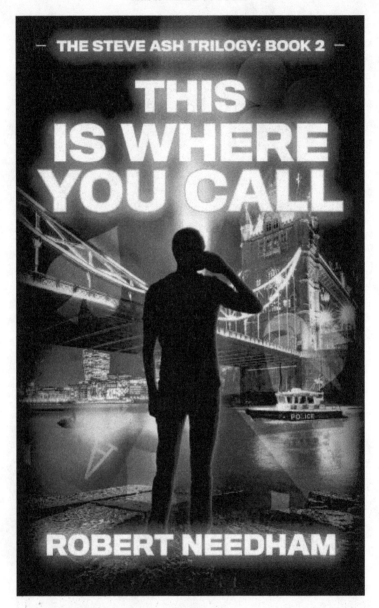

THE STEVE ASH TRILOGY: BOOK 2

THIS IS WHERE YOU CALL

ROBERT NEEDHAM

Trapped by the technology he designed, Steve Ash finds

himself cheating at poker for the mob. But an unexpected meeting offers him a way out. Will Steve risk his own life, and the lives of his family to escape his tormentors?

When Steve is singled out by the NCA as someone with the potential to be an informant, Steve begins to work as a double agent, cheating at Poker for the mob, whilst providing information to the police. The deeper he gets, the more Steve finds himself facing the dilemma of double-crossing people he's befriended, to bring down members of a thriving criminal underworld.

Will Steve be able to fly under the radar, or will his bluff be discovered?

This is Where You Call is the second book in the Steve Ash Trilogy, and the latest instalment in Robert Needham's Poker Crime Thriller series. If you like the adrenaline of a car chase, the subterfuge of James Bond and a gripping tale with heroes on both sides, then you'll love Robert Needham's sequel to This is Where You Fold.

Buy This is Where You Call today, to read Robert Needham's latest thriller in the Steve Ash Trilogy.

Authors Notes

I hope you enjoyed reading This is Where You Fold as much as I enjoyed writing it. It is incredibly difficult to cheat in any legitimately run game. Casinos are strictly regulated and even an accusation of a casino running an illegitimate operation could be incredibly damaging to their business.

Some of the hands in the book are based on hands that happened in real life, either one's I have found on YouTube whilst doing research, or have happened to me at the felt. Looking back on the book, it feels like a clever way to tell bad beat stories and keep people interested in what I'm saying!

George and Josie are the names of my grandparents. Sadly, Josie did die of Alzheimer's, but George is alive and well, and really does love his historical novels. It gives me great pleasure to put him into a novel of his own.

Get your Free E-book.

Sharkbait is the prequel to 'This is Where You Fold', and follows Grant Johnson as he is incarcerated in Prison. You can get it, by going to robertneedhambooks.com and entering your email address in the form.

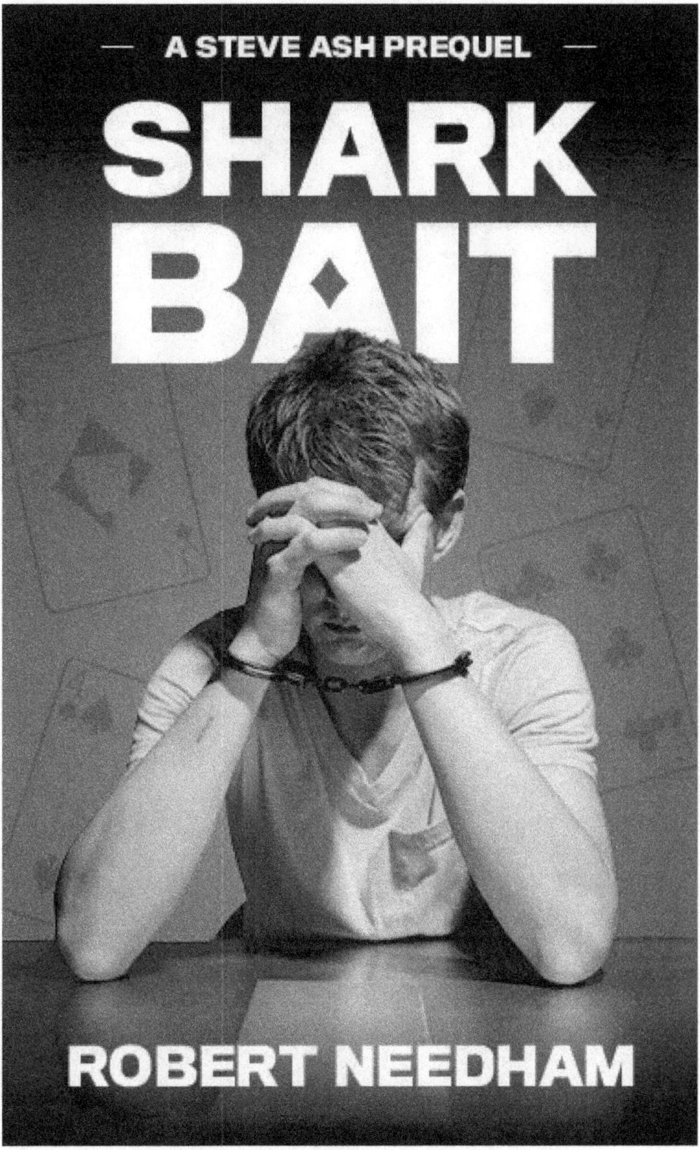
A STEVE ASH PREQUEL
SHARK
BAIT
ROBERT NEEDHAM

When a maths nerd goes to prison, does he have the ability to adapt and survive, or will the brutal environment swallow him up?

One exam away from completing his maths degree, Grant Johnson goes on a boozy night out with classmates and is peer-pressured into buying drugs. With a pocket full of Cocaine, he is refused entry by the bouncers, and then caught by the police, and finds himself facing a sentence of possession with intent to supply. Upon conviction, Grant finds himself thrown into a completely new world where the stakes can be life or death. However, an opportunity to make the best of his predicament appears when he happens upon the prison Poker game. Will he be able to play his way out of trouble, or find himself in too deep?

Sharkbait is the prequel to the highly anticipated poker crime thriller 'The Steve Ash Trilogy'. If you like fast paced action, gritty storylines and a hero to root for, then you'll love Robert Needham's prequel Novella. Get it, by going to robertneedhambooks.com and entering your email address into the form.

You Can Make a Big Difference!

One of the best things about being a writer is having a committed and loyal fan base. As a growing author I am limited by budget in ways that big publishers aren't, and one of the best ways I can grow is for people who have already read my book to leave a review.

Dedication

This book is dedicated to a few people who have helped along the way. Barbara Barnes, for your early encouragement, and going through my first draft with a fine tooth comb. You helped me improve the book immeasurably. Secondly, to my dad, Chris Needham. You've also helped at every stage of the journey, offering advice on way's to improve the story. You've been a great sounding board for the tales of Steve and Grant. Finally, to my wife Christina Needham. I wouldn't have got anywhere near publishing this without you listening to me witter on about plot lines and telling me when I was writing something stupid. You're the best.

Cover Art by Robin Dibben. https://hitop.design/

Edited by Liz Hedgecock https://lizhedgecock.wordpress.com/freelance-writing-and-editing/

About the Author

Robert Needham was born in Wakefield in the UK and has previously worked as a brewer, barman in a cocktail bar, trolley boy in a supermarket and later went on to work for Retail Companies Supply Chain's.

Rob discovered a passion for Poker shortly after graduating university, and on a recent trip to Vegas with his local Poker club, was the only person to come back with a profit.

He is currently writing the Steve Ash Trilogy, the story of a man who finds himself with crippling debt, but uses his tech skills to try and cheat his way out of trouble.

Rob lives in Hertfordshire in the UK with his wife and is due to have a daughter in August.

You can connect with me on:

- https://www.robertneedhambooks.com
- https://twitter.com/RobertNeedham91
- https://www.facebook.com/Robert-Needham-Author-106946677676863

CPSIA information can be obtained
at www.ICGtesting.com
Printed in the USA
BVHW030602121120
593164BV00001B/5